about

Abigail is content with her quiet life as a librarian. But when she's invited to a high-profile charity auction, she finds herself dancing with one of the most beautiful women she's ever met. Abby's sure she'll never see her again, but then Gabrielle calls and asks her on a date. And soon after, another.

Supermodel Gabrielle Levesque has a reputation as the Ice Queen—cold and untouchable—except she warms up whenever she's with Abby. Only Abby isn't interested in the heat between them; she's asexual, and she's worried that admitting as much to Gabrielle might spell the end of their blooming romance.

They're two different women from two very different worlds, but Abby knows she can love Gabrielle. Her passion for books, travel, and theater prove there's more to the Ice Queen than meets the eye. But they'll have to overcome Abby's fears—and Gabrielle's own threatening secrets—in order to find their way to love.

Riptide Publishing
PO Box 1537
Burnsville, NC 28714
www.riptidepublishing.com

Thaw

Cover art: Natasha Snow, natashasnowdesigns.com
Editor: Carole-ann Galloway
Layout: L.C. Chase, lcchase.com/design.htm

ISBN: 978-1-62649-514-2

First edition
April, 2017

Also available in ebook:
ISBN: 978-1-62649-513-5

seasons of love
book two

ELYSE
SPRINGER

RIPTIDE
PUBLISHING

You are not broken. You are not alone. You are perfect exactly the way you are.

And you are loved.

table of Contents

c h a p t e r

One

"Hold still."

The order was tinged with fondness, and Abby forced herself to stop squirming.

"How do people do this every day?" she asked. "I thought cruel and unusual punishment was banned in this country."

An exasperated sigh was all she got in response. Abby glanced up to see Sara watching her, mouth frowning but eyes soft. Abby immediately felt guilty for being so difficult; they weren't really friends, and Sara was doing her a favor tonight. "Sorry," she said meekly.

Sara brushed her hair behind her ears and tilted her head, tapping an eyeliner pencil against her thigh as she waited. "I have to get ready for work in half an hour," she said. "I'm going to leave you as-is if I don't finish. You'll look lopsided all night."

It would have been a threat if Abby had been invested in the process in the first place. But she took a deep breath and settled down into silence again.

For a whole minute.

"Okay, nope. I'm drawing the line. You are not using that torture device on me."

Sara peered down at the silver contraption in her hand. "It's an eyelash curler."

"It's a Medieval favorite of the Spanish Inquisition," Abby responded.

Sara seemed to weigh her options for a moment, then clearly decided it wasn't a battle worth waging. "Fine," she said. "Lips, and then you're done."

Lips involved yet another pencil, and a lipstick that made Abby's lips look *huge*. She made a kissy face at the mirror, taking in the stranger staring back at her. "I don't think I've worn makeup like this since my high school prom."

"You went to prom?" Sara's voice rose in surprise.

"Yeah, of course I did," Abby said, and so what if she sounded a bit petulant? She didn't add that she'd only gone because she'd wanted to fit in, because her mother had made sad eyes in her direction whenever she'd thought Abby wasn't watching, probably wondering what was wrong with her daughter who didn't seem to belong.

Sara looked mildly ashamed. "Sorry," she said. "I didn't mean to imply . . ."

"It's fine." Abby was used to it; mousy, bookish librarians weren't expected to be social butterflies, after all.

"Let's get you dressed." Sara seemed intent on changing the subject, and Abby let her lead them to the bedroom, where several dresses lay across the hastily-made bed. "I grabbed three out of my closet. You're a couple of inches shorter than me, but it shouldn't matter too much since you'll be in heels."

Ugh. "Don't remind me," Abby grimaced. She glanced down at the dresses, each one with more lace and sparkles than the one before it. Nothing in her own closet would compare. "I don't know where to begin?"

Sara looked her over. "You can pull off something shorter, with legs like those," she said. Abby flushed pink, and Sara laughed. "Come on, live a little. This is your one Cinderella moment. Getting dressed up, having a handsome date to the ball. Maybe you'll find a Prince Charming."

"I'm telling Nathan that you called him handsome," Abby joked.

"I will deny it to my dying breath," Sara returned easily. She picked up a black dress that had less actual fabric than some of Abby's swim suits. "Try this one. And quickly, Nathan will be here with the car in fifteen."

The dress was soft. Silky. The material clung against her skin and made her ultra-sensitive to every draft in the small apartment. She studied herself in the mirror, beanpole skinny and freckles over her shoulders, and tried in vain to tug the dress down lower on her thighs.

Sara let out a low whistle. "Damn, girl," she said. "If I wasn't straight, I'd tap that."

Abby blushed again. "It's too short."

"It's perfect," Sara insisted. "Shoes, quickly, and we'll touch up makeup and hair and get you out of here right on schedule."

The heels were black pumps, as sleek and fashionable as the dress. Abby took tottering baby-deer steps in them, trying to find her balance, while Sara fussed over her hair.

Abby's phone buzzed on the dresser. She grabbed it and read the message. "Nathan's five minutes out.".

Sara rocked back on her heels and smiled. "You're going to blow them away tonight."

"I'm still not sure why I'm going to this in the first place."

"Because I couldn't get out of working tonight, and Jason is in Philly on a business trip until Sunday."

Her friend Nathan had stopped in at the library three days before, panicked and desperate. The charity auction was a big deal, and he was expected to go since the play he was currently starring in was a major contributor to the foundation. He was still reeling from the success of the play, and from his own leap into the spotlight, but he'd become a good friend to Abby— One of the few she had.

"I'm not sure I can do this on my own," he'd said, leaning over the reception desk. "I'm no good with people."

"Bull," Abby had responded. "You're great with people. You just aren't good at being *yourself* with people. Put on a role, and you're fine. Why isn't Jason going to this thing with you? I thought champagne and suits would be right up his alley."

Nathan had frowned. "Business trip. The office in Philadelphia is having some kind of big audit, and he'll be there all weekend helping to get it sorted." He'd turned those big blue eyes on her. "Will you be my date to the ball, Abigail?"

And Abby had been weak. Weak and defenseless against Nathan's charm and weapons-grade gaze. "Fine," she said. "But there had better be some good quality booze at this thing, is all I'm saying."

And now here she was, powdered and painted and in a dress that covered less skin than she was really comfortable with, feet already sore in the heels while she waited on the curb for the black car to pull up and a driver to come around and open the door for her.

She slid onto the cool leather seat next to Nathan.

"Holy shit, lady," he said. "Look at you!"

Was blushing going to be a thing tonight? Abby's cheeks grew hot. "You look pretty good yourself."

The first time she'd met Nathan, he'd been dressed like a disheveled street kid. It had been blowing snow and ice outside, and he'd slipped into the library with no hat or gloves to warm up for a few minutes. Those blue eyes had been dim with pain then, and his shoulders had been slumped as though the weight of the world was pressing down on them.

Now, though, he was completely different. His back was straight, eyes bright and lips twitching in a constant smile. He'd turned his life around, and it showed.

"I mean it, Nate," she said quietly. "You look really good."

His grin softened into something genuine. "I feel really good," he said. "We've sold out the entire run, and they're talking about adding more shows through the end of the year. And Jase and I . . . things are really good."

Abby touched his arm. "Good," she echoed. "Now, tell me all about this fancy party that you're dragging me to tonight."

She let Nathan ramble on as the car navigated the evening traffic over the bridge into Manhattan. The party was also a silent auction, a way for the wealthiest echelon of New York City to upstage one another in a game of who-can-spend-the-most. That fact that it was for HIV/AIDS research was apparently irrelevant to them. "These guys don't care about the disease. But we're still going to raise a lot of money for a good cause." Nathan smiled. "Plus, the food should be excellent, and there will be dancing."

Abby wasn't convinced, and gave Nathan a raised eyebrow.

"Did I mention that it's open bar?" he added.

"Oh, thank goodness," Abby breathed, laughing.

They spent the rest of the ride catching up. Nathan had been busy, his off-Broadway production of RENT getting rave reviews in the month since it had opened. They took turns filling each other in on their jobs and lives: Abby told him stories about weird people she encountered while working at the library, and then Nathan caught her up on his relationship with Jason.

Finally, the car slowed and pulled over, and she looked out the window to the lit-up building. "Let's do this thing."

The driver opened the door to help her out, and Abby miraculously made it onto the sidewalk without embarrassing herself. It was early April, but the spring evening was still cold enough that she shivered, wrapping her coat around her shoulders. Nathan joined her and offered her his elbow, escorting her into the gala.

Inside was almost blindingly bright, jewelry glimmering under chandeliers and waiters in starched shirts and black ties weaving effortlessly through the crowds. They checked their coats and Nathan led her in a beeline for the nearest waiter, grabbing two flutes of champagne before they'd even paused to catch their breath.

"I'm so glad you understand me," Abby said, taking a sip.

"Trust me, I'm not sure I can do this without a little social lubrication either." Nathan held his glass out to her. "Cheers, and thanks for being my date tonight."

Abby clinked their glasses together, the sound tiny in the loud room. She went to take another sip, but her eyes caught on a figure in red across the room. A woman stood there, out of place in a sea of more neutral tones. She was clearly angry, gesturing tersely to the man standing in front of her. She looked . . . stunning. Radiant. Abby hadn't realized that someone could be so furious and so beautiful at the same time.

The woman turned in her direction, and Abby glanced away quickly, taking a bigger gulp of her drink than she'd planned and coughing as the bubbles caught in her throat.

"Woah, easy," Nathan said. "You alright?"

Abby blinked as her eyes watered, and she managed a smile. "Yeah, I'm fine." Her eyes darted back over, but the woman in red had stormed off, leaving the man alone. She shifted her gaze back to Nathan, refocusing. "So, tell me more about the run extension for the play."

P arties were . . . not Abby's thing. She wasn't a fan of the noise, of socializing, or of getting dressed up for just a few short hours. But Nathan seemed to be enjoying himself, shaking hands with theater patrons and donors and taking complements about his performance with a light blush and blinding smile.

"You seem like you're completely bored," someone said, stopping by her elbow with a glass of something amber held loosely between two fingers.

Abby looked around.

"Yeah, talking to you," the guy said, sounding amused. "You came with Nathan, right? I saw you walk in together, but was too busy schmoozing with some bigwigs to come say hi." He shifted the glass to his other hand and held his free hand out to shake. "I'm Tony, one of the directors for the Rent production."

"Oh!" Abby shook his hand, flustered. "Sorry. Abigail. Nathan's just a friend, we didn't come together. *Together* together, I mean. Obviously I'm his plus-one tonight." She clamped her lips shut, cheeks burning.

Tony laughed, seeming unfazed by her nervous rambling. "I figured. So what did he have to blackmail you with to get you to fill in tonight?"

"He just asked."

"And you said yes? Clearly you had no idea what you were getting into." Tony gestured around the room with his drink, then took a sip. "I hate these things. Sucking up to people with too much money, trying to get them to part with some of their trust fund to help people who are barely scraping by. Pasting on a smile and pretending like I'm enjoying my fifty-dollar plate consisting of an artistically placed green bean and a sliver of steak."

Abby relaxed as Tony spoke. "I got two green beans."

Tony put on a wounded look that would do any of his actors proud. "Two? I feel cheated. Where's the event planner? I want to file a complaint."

"At least the drinks are free," Abby pointed out.

"The saving grace of the entire night," Tony agreed easily. "So really, how bored are you? I think the only people who want to be here tonight are the rich folks with the big pocketbooks, and the rest of us just have to grin and bear it. Though Nathan looks like he's managing to enjoy himself at least." They both looked over to where the blond hair peeked out from a crowd of older women who sparkled under the lights like they'd robbed a Tiffany's.

Abby shrugged. "It's alright. I like to people-watch. Make up stories in my head about them."

Tony drained the last of his drink and set it down on an empty table. "Do you dance?" he asked suddenly. "I haven't danced in ages. Come keep me company on the floor for a bit, and tell me stories about the people around us."

Abby opened her mouth to protest, but he was already leading her out onto the dance floor, pausing once they'd stopped to twirl her effortlessly before settling a hand on her hip. She finally managed to say, "I don't really know how to dance."

"It's easy." Tony took her hand, pulling her closer, and then smiled reassuringly. "Just follow my lead. Nothing fancy." He led them further into the crowd. "Tell me about those two. The older couple over there, him with the gray suit and her in the dark blue dress."

Following his gaze, Abby smiled. She'd been watching them before, both of them frail and white-haired. "They've been together for sixty years at least," she said, the story already unraveling in her mind. "Both of them genuinely love theater, they fund as many projects as they can and go to shows twice a week. After the shows they have coffee and hold hands as they walk home."

Tony was smiling, a hint of sadness in his eyes. "That's the dream, isn't it?" He shook his head, then nodded at a woman in painful-looking heels, hair piled up high on her head. She was dancing stiffly with a handsome young man. "How about them?"

Abby didn't even need to think. "Marriage for convenience, not love," she said. "She got a rock the size of the Hope Diamond out of it, and he gets a trophy wife. They're only here to show off her new nose job and for him to brag about his recent investment payoffs. The sex is lousy, and they'll divorce within two years."

Tony turned them, dipping Abby playfully. She glanced over her shoulder, and spotted a flash of red. Surprise must have shown on her face, because Tony looked over to see what had caught her eye.

"Oh," he said. "I know all about *her*. No need to create a fiction for that one."

Abby watched the woman through the crowd of dancers. She was dancing with the same man that she'd been arguing with before, face blank and body stiff. He seemed to be enjoying himself though, hand sliding down her waist. "Tell me her story," she said.

Tony spun them so they could both see the woman in red. "They call her the Ice Queen. Complete bitch, if you'll pardon my language. But talented, and she knows it, which makes the attitude even harder to deal with. She's been on and off stage for years, but rumor has it that she's switched to modelling now."

Abby could see why the nickname had stuck. She was like an iceberg: beautiful, but probably deadly if you got too close. "I can see why she'd model," she said instead.

Tony didn't say anything for a second. When she turned back, he was watching her with a soft smile. "If I said that I'd rather look at you than watch her, how cheesy would you rate that?"

The blush was back in full force. "I'm . . ." Abby stared down at the floor. "I'm flattered?"

"You don't sound too sure."

Abby shook her head, biting her lip and shifting awkwardly in Tony's arms.

"Can I take you out sometime?" The question surprised Abby. She wasn't the type of woman who was asked out by handsome men at parties. But Tony sounded genuinely interested. Doubt must have shown on her face, because he continued. "It's just . . . you're gorgeous, and funny, and Nathan talks about you and how you get really excited when you talk about a new book, and I'm intrigued. I'd like to learn more."

Abby looked up, eyes wide. "I don't . . . I'm not . . ." she bit her lip to stop herself from speaking further, and if the heat in her cheeks got any stronger she might actually combust.

"Hey, what are you saying to put a look like that on her face?" Nathan sailed in—*to the rescue*, Abby's mind supplied—appearing at Tony's shoulder with a grin. "Do you mind if I cut in? Janine is searching for you, said it's important."

Tony hesitated, as though he might object, but the importance of business with his co-director eventually won. He leaned forward, kissing Abby on the cheek. "Thanks," he said. "For the dancing, and for the stories. Let me know if you're interested in getting coffee sometime, alright?"

He passed Abby over to Nathan, and patted Nate on the shoulder before cutting through the crowd to find their other director. Abby's shoulders relaxed, tension draining as Nathan took her in his arms. "You alright?" he asked.

"Yeah, I'm fine," Abby said. She let Nathan lead her in silence for a second. "Tony asked me out."

"I had a feeling that was the case." Nathan tried turning her, laughing when they both stumbled a bit. "Sorry, I'm not as smooth as Tony is. Jason's been attempting to teach me, but I usually follow. Why didn't you just tell him that you're not interested in guys?"

"What?" Abby stopped dead on the dance floor, and only Nathan's hand on her hip got her moving again. She gaped at him.

Nathan seemed flustered. "Sorry," he said. "I just assumed? I mean, I wasn't sure, but I guessed, and . . . oh, crap. Sorry. I know what they say when you assume."

"No, it's true. Mostly." Abby studied the pattern on his tie to avoid looking directly at him. "For the most part, I'm more attracted to women than men, but I don't really . . . date? Or anything. I'm not . . ."

"Hey, you don't need to tell me. Whatever you're comfortable with, all good. I didn't mean to put you in an awkward place."

Abby shook her head. "It's alright," she said. "I don't usually talk about it. How'd you guess, though? About the women?"

Nathan laughed against her cheek. "It's the way you watch people," he said. "I can always tell when you find someone interesting, and you linger over the women longer than the men."

"Oh." Abby pulled back to look at him, but there was no judgement.

"Anyways, Tony's going through his own shit right now, from what I've heard. I suspect he's had a bit too much to drink tonight. Remind me someday to tell you about the first time we met."

"Thanks." Abby squeezed his arm and smiled. "For the rescue."

Nathan wrapped her up in a hug right there in the middle of the dancers. "Of course."

chapter Three

The party was finally winding down, and the big clock on the wall said it was well past midnight. *Time to turn into a pumpkin*, Abby thought. She wriggled her toes in her shoes, wondering if she would ever get the feeling back in her feet.

Nathan was talking with some of the other actors across the room, and a few dancers still lingered on the floor, not quite ready to give up on the night and head home. Abby sighed, swallowed down a yawn, and dug her nails into her palms to avoid rubbing her eyes and smudging the makeup.

An arm wound around her own, startling her awake, and she looked over to see a flash of red before she was suddenly being turned. "Dance with me," a woman's voice said.

"Excuse me?" Abby tried to pull away, but the grip on her arm was firm. Then there was a soft body pressed against hers, and red. So much red, filling her vision.

The Ice Queen.

"Please, I'm begging you. Just for a moment." The woman had an accent, just barely noticeable beneath the clipped words. "I'll pay you back for this. Just, I need you to dance with me. One song.."

Abby pulled back far enough to study her abductor. It was the woman in the red dress, certainly, but she didn't have the fierce radiance from before. Instead she seemed . . . tired. A little sad. Something in her eyes said that she might even be desperate, and Abby found herself swallowing her objections and nodding.

"Okay. Only for a few minutes though."

The woman relaxed against her. "Thank you."

They moved in silence for a while, bodies swaying to the music.

The woman was warm, the smooth skin of her bare arms making Abby shiver when it brushed against her own. She tried to take in as much detail as possible; skin a shade of brown that was clearly natural, not artificial, eyes so dark that they were almost black. Flawless skin, makeup highlighting features that were already stunning.

"You're staring." The woman shifted, and a hand brushed against the small of Abby's back, touch light but sensual.

It was definitely a blushing night. "Sorry."

"No need to apologize. I think staring is the least of the payments you can demand from me right now."

"Will you tell me why you're so desperate for a dance?" Abby asked.

The woman turned her wordlessly, so Abby could see across the room. It took her only a second to spot the man glowering at them from one of the tables. She glanced away quickly, rotating the rest of the way around until the man was out of sight again.

"My manager," the woman said.

"He doesn't look at you like he's just your manager."

The woman gave a sharp smile, but there was no humor in it. "And so you see why I was so desperate to escape for a few minutes."

"Oh." And what else could she say?

"What's your name, little rabbit?" The woman pulled Abby closer, brushing their cheeks together and speaking low words against Abby's ear. "What should I call my rescuer this evening?"

"A-Abby," she stuttered. She could feel Gabrielle against her, around her, warm and soft, and it made her shiver. "I mean. Abigail."

The woman gave her another tiny smile, but this time it reached her eyes. "Abigail." With that faint accent, the word sounded like a caress instead of just a name. "Thank you again. I do owe you."

"What's yours?"

"My name?" The woman seemed almost surprised to be asked that, as though it wasn't a question she heard often. Abby remembered what Tony had said. "*They call her the Ice Queen.*" This was someone who had a reputation. Someone Abby would know if she really belonged here tonight. "Please call me Gabrielle."

Her accent became more pronounced when she said her name, French to Abby's untrained ear.

"And ah," Gabrielle said. "There we go." She pulled away ever so slightly, and the air that rushed between them felt cold after being surrounded by such tenderness. Gabrielle turned Abby again, in time for Abby to see the glaring man get up and stalk off in the direction of the restroom. "He's had too much to drink tonight. It was only a matter of time."

As they finished the rotation, Abby turned her head to watch the man vanish from the room. She glanced back at Gabrielle, opened her mouth to ask a question, then closed it.

Gabrielle appeared more alive than she had before, eyes bright and features relaxing, as though every inch between her and her manager gave her more energy. "And now, *mon lapin*, I'm afraid I need to leave you. Thank you for the dance."

"Wait!" Gabrielle had taken a step back, but paused when Abby spoke. "You're leaving?"

"I have a chance to make my escape. I'll have to be quick, and hope I can get to the car before he returns. Sometimes it is better to retreat from battle than to continue fighting, but I am sure I will have my victory in the end." She looked Abby over, taking her in from head to toe, and tapped a manicured finger against her lips. Then she smiled, sharp and calculating. "I believe I owe you a proper thank you. Give me your number."

Abby blinked. "I don't have a pen."

"I'll remember it."

And that was one Abby had heard before. A brush-off, a polite method of extending the fiction a bit longer until Gabrielle could go on her way and forget that she had ever met Abby and danced with her.

"Abigail." Gabrielle's eyes bored into Abby's own with an intensity that made Abby's mouth dry. She brushed a hand along Abby's jaw, cupping it and holding her gaze. "I will remember. I swear it."

Abby rattled off the number before she could stop herself.

Gabrielle gave her a real smile now, one that made her eyes shine and thawed her, if only for a second. "Thank you." She took Abby's hand, placing a kiss on the back of it like a scene from an old black-and-white film. "And now I *really* must go. Goodnight, Abigail."

She turned, a flare of red silk and long black hair, and swept out the door, leaving Abby alone on the dance floor.

"What the hell just happened?" Abby muttered to herself.

She glanced around, half expecting everyone to be staring at her, or to see the entire place had transformed while she'd been absorbed in Gabrielle's words and in her arms. But no one was looking at her, and no one seemed to have noticed the famous model dancing with a nobody librarian.

No, not no one. The man had just walked back into the room, Gabrielle's manager. He was glaring at Abby from the doorway. Abby swallowed, quickly exiting the dance floor and putting as much distance between herself and the man as she could. She spotted Nathan sitting at a table with a couple of women from the play that Abby had met a handful of times before, and felt a rush of relief as she hurried to join them.

The two women seemed to take Abby's appearance as a sign to stretch and say their goodbyes. "It's late," one of them said. "You both have a good night. Nate, see you tomorrow afternoon at the theater."

Nathan nodded and waved goodbye, then slid a glass of water over to Abby, who took it gratefully. "So. You and the Ice Queen, hm?"

"Don't call her that. Her name is Gabrielle." Abby gripped the glass, the words more forceful than she'd intended. She took a gulp of the cold liquid, her body going hot with embarrassment.

Nathan seemed startled by her vehement response. "Sorry. I knew that. It's just . . . she's not a nice person, Abby. Beautiful and talented, but cruel. At least that's what everyone says."

Cruel? "She seemed a bit distant, sure. But not mean. We only danced and talked for a few minutes, but she was nice. Charming."

"Just be careful." Nathan didn't seem convinced. "I've never met her before tonight, but the theater community passes gossip faster than a group of eighty-year-old yentas. Her name comes up a lot. And rarely in a good way."

Abby nodded, but Nathan's words didn't make sense. She'd seen Gabrielle up close, had talked with her. And then the image from the first time she'd seen Gabrielle that evening flashed through her mind . . . a vengeful goddess, fury palpable. Abby shivered in the warm room. "Okay, I'll be careful. But it's not like I'll ever see her again. This is your world, Nate, not mine."

Nathan nodded. "Probably for the best. I don't want you to get hurt."

"I'm a big girl," Abby stated. "I can take care of myself."

Nathan laughed humorlessly. "Yeah, I thought that about myself for a while. Just . . . let me care at least. You're a friend, and I worry about you dancing and having feelings for a woman that's earned a nickname like the Ice Queen."

He had a point. "Alright, I'll be careful. You ready to go? It's long past midnight, and our carriage awaits so I can turn back into a normal girl and get out of these princess clothes."

Nathan stood easily, too much energy after such a late night. He helped Abby to her feet while he spoke. "Yeah, let's blow this joint. I'm crashing at Sara's tonight if you want to come over for cheap Merlot and slice-and-bake cookies."

Abby thought about it for a moment. She hadn't really had friends before Nathan had barged into her library and her life at the beginning of the year. Now she had Nathan, who texted her daily and stopped by to say hello whenever he was in the area to hang out with Sara. And she had Sara and Jason, too, smiling and cheerful faces who were slowly moving from friends-of-friends to people she actually cared about.

But sometimes it was too much, and she needed her alone time. Right then, the thought of spending hours with Nathan and Sara, talking and probably watching movies, sounded exhausting. "I think I'm just going to head home. Does your driver mind dropping me off? And I'll get Sara's clothes back to her over the weekend."

Nathan nodded. "Of course. It's been a long night."

Abby followed him out to the curb, waited while their hired car pulled up and sank tiredly into the soft seats. A long night, yes, and also a weird one. Being asked out by Tony, dancing with Gabrielle. The angry man staring at her across the room, as though she'd conspired to let a prisoner escape from jail instead of dancing with a beautiful woman for a few brief moments.

"Penny for your thoughts?" Nathan asked as the car drove through the still-crowded Manhattan streets.

"Gotta offer at least a dollar. Inflation sucks."

"They better be some good thoughts." Nathan nudged her gently.

"You had a strange look on your face just then."

Abby thought about explaining. She thought about spilling the entire conversation with Gabrielle, telling him what had happened and how her manager seemed like the cruel one. But then she remembered how casually Nathan had thrown out that phrase, *Ice Queen*, and the desire to share dried up. "It's nothing . . . Just tired. You mind if I doze a bit while we drive?"

Nathan pulled out his phone, probably to text Jason despite the late hour. "Nah, go for it. Feel free to use my shoulder, though Sara says it's a pretty bony pillow."

"Thanks." Abby closed her eyes, and recalled the vision of red silk and black hair and eyes that held fire.

c h a p t e r

Four

A bby loved working at the library. She loved being around books all day, talking to patrons about upcoming releases and handing out recommendations to kids who still found libraries magical. She'd gone to school for a Masters in Library Science, even though her mother had tried to talk her out of it.

"Libraries won't even be around in a few years," she'd said. "They're always talking about closing the one near me. You're spending thousands to get a job that you'll have for maybe a decade?"

But Abby had ignored her, had gone to grad school and walked away with a shiny piece of paper that certified her to sit around and talk books for eight hours a day.

Worth it, she thought, as she handed three chapter books to an excited girl. The girl's mom waved, and Abby grinned and waved back as they headed out into the sunshine.

The library was fairly busy this afternoon, the sun shining and bringing people out of their homes as spring took hold on the city. Abby helped a couple of seniors with suggestions for their book club, and located a DVD in the return bin that a young man had been desperate to find so he could impress his girlfriend. There was a man her own age using the computer in the corner to search for a job, and a woman her mother's age doing genealogy research, paperwork spread across two computer desks.

"Anyone who says libraries are useless should shut their mouth," she said out loud.

Her co-worker Brian gave her a look, but he was used to her speaking her thoughts with no prompting. "Yeah, but instead they come in at nine o'clock on a Tuesday morning and wonder why the only person in the entire building is that homeless guy who lives in the park."

"If they'd talk to Gus, they'd know that he's actually incredibly brilliant," Abby said. She'd spent an hour on a slow winter morning once, talking to him about Kant and free will until her head was spinning.

Brian was checking books in behind her, slowly wading through the stack that had built up that afternoon. "So I guess you've heard the news then?".

Abby waved hello to an older woman she recognized, probably coming in for the latest Nora Roberts. "What news?"

"You mean you don't know?" Brian stopped what he was doing, a DVD held in one hand and the scanner in the other. "The way you were talking just now, I figured you'd heard."

Abby plucked the DVD out of his hands and checked it in on her own computer. "Just spill already," she said. "The suspense is killing me."

"The budget cuts," Brian said. "They're talking about closing down a few branches before the beginning of summer."

"Oh, that." Abby rolled her eyes and grabbed another stack to help Brian out. They'd be here all night at this rate, and she had plans to watch Netflix with her feet up this evening. "It's the same thing as last quarter, and the quarter before that."

"Abby." Brian's voice dropped, his tone serious enough to make her pause and glance back over. "They have a list this time. Of half a dozen libraries that they want to close." He looked grim. "Our branch is on it."

The book in her hands was set down carefully. "A list?" she said. They'd always threatened to close branches around the city, always complained about how there wasn't enough in the budget, but they'd always found the money before. But the city had never come up with a list until now. "Where'd you hear this?"

"It was in the paper this morning. Give me a second to find it." Brian pushed to his feet, check-in pile abandoned, and slid out from behind the counter to track down a copy of that day's *Times*. When he came back, he had the article folded over for Abby to read.

BUDGET PROPOSAL INCLUDES CLOSING LIBRARIES

The article was pretty short and buried in one of the back pages beneath an article about a new tax proposal. But like Brian had said, there were six branches listed, with the reporter saying the city wanted them closed by mid-June in an attempt to save the second half of the year's budget.

"Well shit," Abby said.

"Language," Brian said, but he sounded like he'd like to be dropping a few four-letter words, too. "I called a friend in Queens over lunch. His co-worker is pregnant and thinking about quitting to be a stay-at-home mom. I might be able to transfer over when she goes, if this comes to pass."

Abby's thoughts were racing. "I could ask a few people," she said, "but there are more librarians in this city than there are positions."

"Jersey City is hiring," Brian pointed out.

Abby rolled her eyes and wrinkled her nose, letting her expression what she thought of *that* suggestion.

A couple of patrons looked like they were starting to wander over to the counter, so Abby set the paper aside and switched her smile back on, greeting them as they approached and chatting about their finds while she checked them out.

But her mind was reeling. *Close down the library?* They had plenty of people coming in every day, and they were in a great location, only a few blocks from two schools. What would the people in the neighborhood do if the branch closed? The next closest library was a twenty-minute bus ride at least, and much smaller.

"This could blow over, just like it has every time before," Abby said when the last person in line had gone on their way.

Brian didn't even glance up from the materials he was checking in. "Sure, you keep thinking that. I'm going to call my friend in Queens again tomorrow and see if he can put in a good word for me."

Abby tried to force a cheerful exterior for the rest of the day, but as they were finishing up their shift and collecting all of the books that had been left around, she found her smile slipping. Alone in the aisles, with no one around, the smile vanished and she tried to calm her panic as she set books back into their homes on the shelves.

This is what my mother warned me about, she thought, followed immediately by, *Oh, crap, I'm going to have to hear the* I told you so *speech from my mom.* That thought was more terrifying than that of actually losing her job, and she quickly banished it for more pleasant thoughts . . . like homelessness and being unemployed at age twenty-nine.

Librarians didn't get paid well, and she didn't exactly have a savings cushion to help her out if the worst did come to pass. But there were always options, so she just needed to be careful and budget over the next few months, so she could afford a few rent checks if she did find herself searching for work.

"I'm heading out," Brian called from a few aisles over. "You want to walk to the station with me?"

Abby still had a full cart to shelve, having been too lost in her thoughts to work as quickly as she normally did. "Nah, I need to finish this up before I leave or the ladies on the evening shift will be grumpy," she said. "Have a good night! I'm off tomorrow, but I'll see you on Friday!"

She heard Brian leave through the back, and let the silence surround her for a minute before taking a deep breath and letting the tension drain out of her. "It's going to be okay." Saying the words out loud seemed to help. "It'll be fine. It's just another scare, just the suits trying to wring every last cent they can out of the city."

Her phone and earbuds were tucked in her sweater pocket, so she pulled up her streaming app and put some music on while she finished off her tasks. That helped her focus on something other than her winding thoughts, and it was less than an hour later before she was waving goodbye to the group of librarians who worked until the library closed at nine and stepping out into the afternoon sunshine.

Thank you, Daylight Savings. The world was hazy and orange, and the city smelled nice for once, the trees lining the street bringing a fresh scent to layer over the smog.

Abby kept the music playing while she walked to her bus. Her phone buzzed in her pocket at one point, but the bus was crowded and she wasn't up for maneuvering around to dig it out. Instead she people-watched, tucked up in her seat against the window. People on the bus heading home from work, people on the sidewalk getting groceries from the bodega or walking dogs.

A flash of red caught her eye, and her head whipped around,

startlingthe man sitting next to her.

But of course it wasn't anything. A jogger in a bright red shirt, oblivious to Abby's neuroses. She sagged back against the seat.

It had been four days since the charity auction. Four days since she'd danced until her feet ached, and ended the night in the arms of a stunning woman who had promised to call her. But she'd known then that Gabrielle's promise to call was too good to be true, and time had proven her right.

Her stop came up, and Abby squeezed past the crowd of people to get off the bus, taking a deep breath once she was on the sidewalk.

The second-story apartment she shared with her roommante Jenna was blessedly empty when she came in, and Abby dumped her stuff by the door and shuffled into the kitchen to find a bottle of wine and a box of crackers to snack on while she pondered dinner.

Her phone buzzed again in her pocket.

Maybe it's Gabrielle. Her heart raced at the thought.

But Jenna's name popped up on the screen, showing the text that she'd missed while on the bus. Her roommate said she was stopping for takeout on her way home, and did Abby want some? The second text was also from Jenna, asking again.

Abby went to respond with a yes, then paused. "Can't spend money," she said out loud. A disappointment, because takeout sounded heavenly right then.

She texted Jenna with a "thanks, but not tonight" and went to dig out a sad frozen dinner as a consolation prize for not wasting money, tossing her phone on the counter. If the library didn't close, Abby decided, she'd treat herself to a weekend vacation with the extra money. Maybe head to the beach. If—no, *when* the library didn't close.

Her phone buzzed once more while she was sitting on the couch, microwaved pasta in a flimsy plastic dish on her lap. Probably just Jenna again, saying she was on her way home. But the phone was too far away, and Abby had a date with a binge session on the TV.

She was on the second episode when Jenna finally showed up, sans takeout.

"The line at the food truck was a mile long," Jenna said, kicking off her shoes. "I waited, finally got up to the front, and they were out of almost everything. Ended up grabbing a sub on from the deli across the road."

Abby slid over on the couch, making room. "Almost makes me wish the snow would come back."

Jenna grinned. "Almost," she agreed. She unwrapped a sandwich that looked just as unappealing as Abby's pasta had, and Abby dutifully passed over the bottle of cheap wine and extra glass that she'd brought to the living room with her own meal. "Cheers. Man, my day was long. How was yours?"

"Same old." She thought for a second about telling Jenna what the newspaper had said, but something kept her from speaking up. No need to worry her roommate just yet.

They watched an episode of the newest superhero show together, then Jenna stood and stretched. "I'm going to grab my laptop, if you don't mind me watching and working at the same time?"

Abby shook her head.

Jenna took their dinner remnants into the kitchen, and Abby listened to her running water and throwing out their trash. They'd known each other since grad school, although they'd been in different programs, and Jenna had suggested finding a place together after they'd both mentioned wanting to escape their respective awful roommates.

"Hey, Abs, you missed a call on your cell phone," Jenna called from the kitchen.

Abby weighed the pros and cons of getting up from her comfortable spot on the couch. It was probably her mother, and Abby didn't have the energy to deal with her tonight. But if it was from someone at work . . . "Toss it to me?" she called back.

Jenna reappeared just long enough to gently toss the phone towards the couch, and Abby snagged it with only a minor fumble.

One missed call. One voicemail. Unknown number, New York area code.

Abby tapped to play the voice message, and brought the phone up to her ear.

"Hello Abigail. I did say that I would call, and I pray you will forgive me for the unavoidable delay." There was no introduction, but Abby knew that lightly-accented voice, and felt goosebumps rise on her arms. "I would like to take you to dinner on Friday night, if you are amenable. As a thank you, and . . . perhaps as something more?"

The words sounded wistful, fond. "Please let me know, *mon lapin*. I will wait for your call."

chapter
Five

"I need your help."

"You still owe me for the last time." Sara's tone was unimpressed, but she quirked a smile at Abby, softening the words.

But Abby *had* promised to pay Sara back for her help, so she obligingly held out a white plastic bag.

Sara glanced down, opening the bag with a rustle of plastic, and then her eyes widened in surprise. "Well then. You have my attention."

Abby leaned forward. She'd make the run out to her mother's house on Long Island that morning, suffering breakfast with her parents in exchange for an expensive bottle of tequila that her dad had received as a retirement gift and never opened.

"I have a date in a week and a half, and I don't know what to wear."

Sara eyebrows shot up, and she set the bottle of booze aside. "A date? Tell me everything. Who is he? Did you meet at the charity auction?"

Abby hesitated. She was friendly with Sara, and she knew, logically, that Sara wouldn't judge her. After all, Sara's best friend was a gay man. "It's, um. Yeah. I met her at the party on Saturday night. We danced, and she promised she'd call."

"Very Cinderella, I approve." Sara didn't even bat an eye at the pronoun. "Tell me about her. Where's she taking you?"

The conversation with Gabrielle had been teasingly brief, the other woman obviously busy but pleased to take a moment to confirm dinner plans with Abby. "She's taking me to Printemps in Manhattan? Next Friday night. I googled it . . . it's super fancy." *And about a dozen social classes above me*, she added to herself. Her search for the restaurant had turned up more than a few celebrity gossip sites mentioning famous people who had been spotted eating there.

"It has a waiting list a mile long from what I've heard." Sara whistled low. "Damn, who is this lady that can get a table at Printemps on such short notice?"

"Her name is Gabrielle. Nathan said she's been in a few things on Broadway, and that she models now?"

Sara's eyes grew wide. "Gabrielle Levesque?" She took a deep breath. "You're seriously going out with Gabrielle Levesque?"

Abby shrugged. "Maybe?" She hadn't exactly asked for Gabrielle's last name. She pulled her phone out and did a quick search, sounding out the foreign surname. There were thousands of websites, and tens of thousands of images. She clicked on the first thumbnail, and there, in bold color on her tiny phone screen, was the woman she'd danced with on Saturday night. "Yeah, that's her."

"I heard she turned down the lead in *Chicago* to accept a modeling contract with a major fashion company." Sara's voice was hushed with awe.

That revelation made Abby frown. She had known from the start that Gabrielle was too good for her, a model and actor on stage, but a contract with one of the companies on billboards and in fashion magazines? "If she's so famous why would she be taking someone like me out?"

"Well, you're very pretty," Sara said, but her eyes asked the same question.

Abby sighed. "I guess it's just a thank you for helping her out of a situation." The end of Gabrielle's voicemail still lingered in the back of her mind. *And perhaps as something more.* "I thought she meant it as a date, but there's no way she did. I probably read too much into it." After all, they'd only danced together for a few minutes; long enough for Abby to form a crush on an attractive woman, but not long enough for said woman to want to date her.

That seemed to make more sense to Sara, and she looked sympathetic. "Well, you might as well enjoy the night," she said. "I'll help you get dressed up, you'll go to Printemps and have a fantastic dinner that neither of us could ever afford on our own, all with a beautiful woman on your arm for a night." She grinned wickedly. "Hey, who knows, maybe you'll get lucky?"

Abby jolted, and she blushed and shook her head quickly. "Oh, no. I don't . . . she wouldn't—" she stopped mid-sentence, the words stuck in her throat. It took a second for her to manage to speak again. "I'm sure that won't be the case."

"Hey, you can dream!" Sara said, still grinning.

I'll pass on that dream, but thanks. Gabrielle was beautiful, but the idea of going home with her, of Abby stripping off her borrowed clothes and . . . doing anything? Abby shrugged off that thought. "Anyways, you'll help? I'll definitely owe you again."

"For sure. Actually, give me a second to text my friend Laura. She's a makeup artist, and I bet she'll come over and help too."

Abby balked. "I don't need a makeup artist."

Sara didn't pause her fingers, which were flying over the keyboard on her phone. "Look, Abs, you're gorgeous. But you're going out with Gabrielle Levesque on a date to Printemps. You *need* a professional wardrobe consultant and a makeover, but unfortunately that's not going to happen unless you have some serious cash hidden up your sleeve. So let me get Laura over here next week, and we'll raid my closet."

With a flourish, Sara set her phone down on the table and finally focused her attention back on Abby. "What time do you get off work next Friday, and what time is the date?"

"It's not a date." It couldn't be. "I'm off at four thirty and we're meeting at eight. I'll need to take a cab I guess."

"So you'll need to leave here by seven if you hope to make it through Friday night traffic into the city. Not a lot of time, but we'll manage."

Two hours to do hair and makeup and put a dress on? Abby winced. "I'm so definitely not in her league."

"Darlin', not many people in this world are," Sara agreed. "But we're sure as hell going to help you fake it like a pro." Her phone buzzed and Sara glanced down at it. "Awesome, Laura will be here next Friday at five. Get over here as soon as you get off work, alright?"

Abby swallowed around the building panic. "Yeah," she said, voice wavering. "Alright." *What on earth am I getting myself into?*

"What on earth have I gotten myself into?"

Abby set her bag down just inside Sara's door and gaped at the living room table. Or, rather, where the table had once been. Now it was covered by two large boxes and countless tiny items that Abby only vaguely recognized as makeup. Pencils, brushes, black compacts of powder, and another one of those awful torture devices that were supposed to do something amazing (and possibly painful) to your eyelashes.

"Sit." Sara pointed at the couch, then glanced over at a pretty red-haired woman. "Laura's going to start on your makeup, and I'll go bring out the dresses we looked at last night so she can make sure the makeup matches."

Makeup has to match? Abby voiced the words, eyes wide, and got an easy laugh from the woman who must have been Laura. "I'm going to guess you don't wear makeup often," Laura said, coming to sit down on the couch next to Abby.

"No, almost never. Maybe lip gloss if I'm going out with friends?"

Laura nodded. "You have amazing skin. I'm assuming you don't get out in the sun much, either."

"I'm kind of a homebody." Abby shrugged, feeling self-conscious.

"You're lucky." Laura started digging through one of her cases, which was filled with yet more makeup. "Having skin like this means you're less likely to have wrinkles when you're older."

Abby didn't mind the idea of wrinkles. She liked them, actually, especially the little lines next to people's eyes that said they'd spent many years of their life laughing. But she had a feeling Laura would think otherwise.

"These are the two we're thinking of." Sara came back out with a dress in each arm. They'd narrowed the choices down to two from Sara's closet: the first one was black, a longer and sleeker version of the dress she'd worn to the charity auction, while the other was dark red, and the velvety material shifted under the light and made it change as it was turned.

Laura looked them over. "I like the red one," she said finally. "The black will make her look washed out under the restaurant lights, but the red will bring out the little hints of auburn in her hair."

"Awesome, I'll go find shoes to go with it." Sara hung the hanger for the dark red dress over the back of a door, and vanished back to her room, leaving Abby alone with Laura once again.

Laura leveled Abby with a curious stare. "Sara said you're going on a date with Gabrielle Levesque."

"It's not a date," Abby mumbled.

Laura didn't seem to care much about the semantics. "I have such a crush on her," she said. "Woman is *hot*. Lucky you!"

"She's just saying thank you. I helped her out with something, that's all." Abby looked down at her hands in her lap. "Besides, I don't think we'd work out as a couple."

"Who said anything about being a couple?" Laura started grabbing things off the table, seemingly at random, but Laura clearly knew what she was doing. "You let her treat you to dinner, maybe take you home for an amazing one-night stand, and after you can say that you hooked up with Gabrielle Levesque, and then move on with your life." She paused. "I didn't even know she was a lesbian."

Abby twisted her fingers together. "I don't want to have sex with her," she said quietly, but Laura didn't seem to hear.

"Okay, close your eyes and look up. And *don't move.*"

With a sigh, Abby did as she was told, and wondered if it wasn't too late to call and cancel. Sara and Laura both approached sex very casually, talking about hooking up with almost strangers as though it was easy, common. *What if Gabrielle thinks the same thing?* If the other woman wanted to have sex, would Abby say yes? It wasn't that she hated the idea of sex, just . . . she didn't want it. Didn't need it. But no one else ever seemed to feel that way; in high school, college, and even now in the breakroom at work, where some of the part-time ladies would talk about their husbands or dates during lunch, sex was always the focus of every relationship. Laura and Sara were clearly no different, and Abby didn't want to have another conversation where she proved just how weird and different she was. So she kept her mouth shut and eyes closed and tried to think of something else.

The teasing strokes of the brushes on her skin was almost soothing, and Laura and Sara chatted while Abby sat as still as she could, letting Laura's directions guide her.

"Why does she behave for you?" Sara asked. "When I tried to do her makeup a couple of weeks ago it was like pulling teeth to get her to sit still."

Laura laughed and used her thumb to hold Abby's eyelid closed while she smudged eyeliner. "I just have the magic touch."

Sara laughed.

Maybe it's because if I open my mouth, I'm afraid I'll say the wrong thing, Abby thought. She let Sara talk about some guy she'd been on-again/off-again seeing, and noticed that Laura carefully didn't talk about her own relationship, although Abby gathered from the fragments that Laura was dating Sara's ex, and Sara was . . . okay with this? Or rather, not upset about it. The complications of their relationships sounded exhausting, although it was fascinating that there was no apparent jealousy. But then she thought about other relationships she'd witnessed, like Nathan and Jason's, which had been built on deceit and had required a mountain of apologies and pleading in order to reconcile.

This is why I'm glad that I don't date . . . too much drama mixed up in people trying to have sex.

"Yeah, it's usually worth it, at least when you're still in bed!"

Abby's eyes flew open, and she flushed darkly, ignoring Laura's shout to "hold still!"

"I didn't mean to say that," she said. "Sorry."

Laura motioned impatiently for her to stop moving. "Dammit, Sara, don't distract her," she said. "And you, no more sudden movements."

Abby settled back in her seat, closing her eyes once more. Sara and Laura began chatting again, but this time the conversation was all about sex, mostly focused on the mutual acquaintances they had who were sleeping with each other.

Abby kept her mouth shut, grateful for the excuse not to involve herself in the conversation. She didn't want sex, but that concept seemed foreign to the two women sitting in front of her. Still, the thought of having someone to spend time with, to talk to, maybe to hold while she slept? It sounded romantic. *Perfect.* Why was it so difficult for others to contemplate a relationship built on mutual affection, on romantic gestures that didn't extend into the bedroom? Abby wanted roses and inside jokes, something easy and natural. Sex was a complication she didn't have any interest in.

It was another hour before Laura finally stepped back and started packing her makeup boxes back up. "You look amazing," she said.

Sara stood as well. "My turn. Let's get you dressed and do your hair. It's just six now, so I think we should finish in enough time."

They waved goodbye to Laura, and Abby let Sara lead her back to the bedroom to slide the red velvet dress on.

The cab ride into Manhattan was silent. The driver listened to the radio quietly, leaving Abby in the backseat to alternate between watching the lit-up skyline and the ever-rising meter. She kept a tight grip on the small clutch that Sara had loaned her and tried not to do the math. Her bank account was fine now, but that lingering threat of being out of a job made every dollar all the more valuable.

And I'm wasting it on what? A not-date with a woman who's so far out of my league that we're not even playing the same sport anymore?

A voice that sounded suspiciously like Sara's butted in. *Enjoy it. It's one night.*

The cab jerked to the side, passing someone who had decided to slam on their brakes for no apparent reason, and slid easily up to the curb outside of an ultra-modern gray-slate exterior. A tiny sign in green read *Printemps*, but there was no menu out front, no advertising in the windows.

If it weren't for the well-dressed people visible through the window, talking over candlelight and wine, the restaurant would look more like a clothing store or a posh hotel.

She passed over some cash to the driver and climbed out of the cab. The driver pulled away a second later, and Abby was alone on the sidewalk.

She straightened the dress. Touched her hair to make sure it was still in place. Fiddled with the clutch for a second. Thought about pulling her phone out and texting Nathan to come get her; she was in his neck of the woods, if she recalled correctly.

Eventually though, the cold started seeping through her jacket, and she took a deep breath and headed for the restaurant.

A young man opened the door for her before she could reach for the handle. He flashed her a casual smile that most definitely did not say, "I saw you standing there for five minutes looking completely out of place, and I know you don't belong here."

What he did say was, "Welcome to Printemps. May I take your coat?"

Abby handed it over wordlessly, and the man gave her a tiny bow, barely a nod of the head, and vanished with it. A beautiful woman was waiting a few feet away. "Reservation?" she asked.

"Oh. I'm meeting someone. Um, Gabrielle Levesque?"

The hostess nodded calmly, not batting an eye, and motioned for Abby to follow her.

And now Abby could see that she really, truly did not belong. Everyone around her was beautiful, clearly very well-off. They wore jewelry that glimmered, clothing that appeared to be straight off a runway, and—was that man over there the lead actor from that movie she'd watched with Sara and Nathan a few weeks ago? She felt like she was staring, and tore her eyes away from the people in the restaurant to focus on the carpet as she walked.

"Abigail."

A cool voice pulled Abby out of her building panic.

Gabrielle stood, ignoring the hostess to take Abigail's hands in her own. "Thank you so much for coming. Please, have a seat."

They were in the back of the restaurant, a table for two in a nook that felt cozy and almost private. "Thank you for actually calling." Abby blushed. "I mean, for inviting me to dinner. I am glad you called though."

Gabrielle was sitting up straight in her chair, posture perfect. "Of course. It is only fair that I pay you back for the favor you did me."

She had already ordered wine, and a waiter came by to bring Abby a glass as well. He poured a small portion, then waited.

"Taste it," Gabrielle prompted. "Let the gentleman know if this is alright, or if you would prefer something else."

"Oh." Words had escaped her, and Abby had a sinking feeling that she was making a fool of herself. She brought the glass to her nose, smelling it like she'd seen in the movies. It smelled . . . like wine. Was she supposed to smell some kind of flower or wood? She took a sip and immediately set the glass back down. "It's fine," she told the waiter.

He poured the rest of her glass, then left gracefully withdrew to leave them alone again.

Gabrielle was studying her. "It's not fine."

"What?" Abby glanced around. Had she already screwed up?

"The wine." Gabrielle motioned to it. "You made a small face when you sipped it, as though you were displeased."

Oh, crap. The wine probably cost something like a hundred bucks a glass, and Abby had treated it like the five dollar bottles she got at the store on the corner. She pasted on a smile—the same one she used when her mother asked if she liked the pork loin she'd made for dinner, or when Marcy, her boss at the library, asked her to stay late to help put up a new display. "No, it's excellent," she said. "I had a long day at work, and I'm just tired. I apologize."

Gabrielle watched her for another second, then nodded. "Good. I want you to enjoy this evening. Tell me about yourself. Where do you work?"

"At a library in Brooklyn." Abby immediately wished she could take back the words.

Gabrielle's blank exterior shifted minutely, eyes widening. "A librarian," she repeated. She pressed her lips together. "I did not expect that." Her eyes flickered over Abby's dress, the jewelry she'd borrowed.

Of course not, Abby thought, staring intently at the tablecloth. Gabrielle had seen her in an expensive dress at the gala and had probably assumed she was someone who could afford to be there. Had invited her to dinner at Printemps as though she belonged.

"Sorry," Abby said, tracing a pattern on the white cloth with her finger. "I didn't mean to disappoint."

"Quite the opposite, actually." Something is Gabrielle's tone made Abby chance a look up, and she was surprised to see Gabrielle studying her with clear interest. "I am . . . intrigued."

"You are?"

Gabrielle tilted her head, studying Abby without blinking. "Tell me about working at a library."

"Tell you what?" Abby couldn't have heard her correctly.

"I want to know what it's like." Gabrielle's eyes fluttered closed for a second. "Is it a job you love?" Abby spotted a flicker of longing in her face before the expression was replaced again with polite blankness

"Yes, absolutely." Abby didn't hesitate. "I've wanted to be a librarian for as long as I can remember. I've always been a reader." Abby found herself explaining about being a bookworm as a kid, moving from Iowa to Long Island in high school and having books as her friends when she hadn't fitted in at her new school. "I guess that makes me sound like a nerd," she said. "But I've found that books are usually more interesting than other people." She paused, realizing what she'd just said. "Present company excluded, of course."

"Oh, I'm far from interesting," Gabrielle said dismissively. "But I do know what you mean. The magic, the escape from reality. I have turned to books many times when I needed to find escape from the world around me."

"You read?" The words slipped past her lips before Abby's brain-to-mouth filter could catch them. "I mean, you don't look like someone who would . . ." She flushed, mortified. "Sorry."

Gabrielle gave her a smile, the chilly façade reappearing for a moment before fading away again. "I read when I can," she said simply. She must have seen the surprise on Abby's face, and she shrugged. "And you did not expect that, I see. Perhaps we should start fresh, with no expectations."

Abby took a deep breath. Smiled. "Alright," she said. "No expectations."

The waiter returned and Abby realized with a start that she hadn't even looked at her menu. She quickly picked it up, but the entire thing was in French. Across the table from her, Gabrielle drew herself up straight, the warmth vanishing as the waiter interrupted to ask for their order.

Gabrielle motioned for Abby to go first, and her eyes softened. "You do not read French?" She didn't wait for Abby's response. "I apologize. I'll order for us both, if you don't mind?"

Abby nodded mutely.

Gabrielle ordered in fluent French, her tone cool and features blank as she spoke to the waiter. He didn't write anything down, simply nodded and departed as quickly and silently as he'd appeared. Once the waiter was out of sight, Gabrielle relaxed again almost immediately.

"You speak French." Abby mentally slapped her forehead. *Excellent job, Captain Obvious.*

But Gabrielle nodded easily. "I'm from Quebec," she said. "Born and raised, as you say. We learn both English and French in school."

"How did you end up in New York?" Abby leaned forward, curious to hear the answer.

"I went to school in Toronto, then came to New York for further study and to become an actress."

Abby frowned. "There must be more to the story than that!"

Gabrielle thankfully seemed amused, not upset. "As I said before, I am not an interesting person. I have been blessed with good genetics and with a small bit of talent. In this city, that is enough to live on, so I do."

"More than a bit of talent, from what I've heard." Abby said. "Tell me about modeling?"

A strange expression passed over Gabrielle's face, there and gone in a flash. "It's a job," she said simply.

"But one that you don't love."

Gabrielle frowned. "Why do you say that?"

Abby shrugged, turning to peer around the restaurant while she gathered her thoughts. "I like making up stories about people," she said. "It means I watch people a lot. I see what they look like when they're excited, passionate, and enthusiastic about something. But I mention modeling and . . . nothing. You don't react."

Gabrielle sounded surprised. "You have a unique talent for reading people."

"I just love figuring out people's stories," Abby said. "Everyone has at least one inside of them."

The waiter returned before Gabrielle could say anything else, setting a plate in front of each of the women. It was mostly empty except for a small circle of something covered by artfully drizzled sauce and some sprigs of vegetable.

"Fois gras," Gabrielle stated, picking up her fork and knife and holding them delicately.

Abby tried to mimic her, but the utensils felt unwieldy in her hands. She cut into it, took a small bite. It was delicious and the rich flavor exploded over her tongue. "It's fantastic," she said. "I've never had it before."

Gabrielle's smile turned up, and amusement glittered in her eyes. "Do you know what it is?" she asked.

Abby reached for her wine, shaking her head.

"Duck liver."

Abby sputtered on her glass.

Gabrielle laughed. Actually laughed, a delighted sound that seemed to cut through the dim murmuring of their fellow diners. Abby imagined that heads turned in their direction in surprise, but she was too busy watching Gabrielle light up before her.

Stunning. The way Gabrielle's eyes shone, her skin seeming to glow brighter under the lights. It was a complete transformation, and Abby couldn't tear her eyes away.

"It sounds much better in the French, does it not?" Gabrielle didn't seem aware of Abby's thoughts. "I think if someone had simply called it liver the first time I tried it, I would not have been so brave. But *foie gras* sounds much more civilized."

"It does," Abby quickly agreed, gazing back down at her plate before Gabrielle could catch her watching. She set her glass down and fumbled to take another bite. "I've always wanted to go to France, but eating French food sounds terrifying. Frogs legs and snails?"

A man approached Abby from the side as she was waiting for an answer, and Gabrielle's laughter vanished in a split second, turning icy cold, lip curled in disdain. At first Abby thought it was the waiter, back so soon, but the man who spoke was most certainly not their server.

"Gabrielle, darling, so good to see you." The man ignored Abby completely, leaning forward to brush a kiss on Gabrielle's cheeks. She didn't return the greeting, simply blinked slowly, a silent *get on with it please.* "Charming as ever I see," the man continued, chuckling even as the tension at the table grew and Gabrielle's expression didn't change.

Abby studied him. An older man, hair going gray, slightly heavy-set, but wearing a suit that screamed High Fashion and a heavy silver watch.

"I saw you over here, laughing of all things. A surprise, you must understand. I don't know that I've ever seen you crack a smile, but I guess there's a human being under that glare after all." The man talked easily, but every word made Gabrielle tense more, until she looked as though she might shatter beneath it.

"It's very good to see you again, Peter." Gabrielle's tone clearly said the complete opposite. "But I'm afraid you're interrupting an important meeting."

Peter nodded easily, apparently not rebuffed in the slightest by the chilly reception. "Of course, of course." He gave Abby a quick look, taking her in and seeming to dismiss her as irrelevant in a second. "Look, Gabrielle, I heard you were interested in walking the runway during our winter show. I'm still searching for an opener, so you give me a call if you're interested, alright?" The leer he gave her now was decidedly un-business-like. "Maybe we can come to an arrangement like last time."

Gabrielle nodded once, sharply, and finally Peter bussed another kiss on her cheek and took off.

Silence descended on the table, and Abby thought she might choke from the tension Gabrielle was radiating.

"It's only April," She said, searching desperately for a neutral topic. "It seems a little too early to be talking about winter fashion, right?"

Gabrielle didn't relax. "It is.".

More silence.

"You said before that you like to read?" Abby tried again.

This got a small break in the iciness, and Gabrielle's body shifted slightly. "Yes," she said. "It's one of my only escapes. Fiction is a way to break free from reality, is it not?"

"But you must get to travel for your job, right? See the world?" Abby asked.

Gabrielle nodded slowly. "Paris. Milan. London."

"Oh," Abby said, intrigued. "Tell me about them."

But Gabrielle just shook her head. "There is no escape for me in traveling to another city," she said. "I see hotel rooms and dressing rooms. They are not trips for leisure." She seemed to be closing off, the icy exterior returning, so Abby quickly changed the subject back to books

"What do you read then?"

"Fantasy. Science fiction. Those stories which do not take place here on Earth."

"You're a geek," Abby blurted out.

The smile grew, and Gabrielle looked almost pleased.

It was unexpected. Gabrielle Levesque reading Tolkien or Asimov seemed as out of place as Abby herself sitting in the high-class restaurant eating foie gras.

"Is that why you love acting then?" Abby asked.

A complicated series of emotions fluttered over Gabrielle's face, and Abby rushed to catalogue them before they vanished again. Sadness, longing, passion, and something that she thought was bittersweet, a twisting of the lips as Gabrielle closed her eyes for a moment.

"Acting is another escape for me," she said. "Being someone other than myself, being able to forget about my own life and history and take on someone else's problems and hopes and dreams for a few hours, it is like lifting a heavy weight off my chest. And yes, I can immerse myself in a new world and escape in a way that fiction does not quite allow."

Abby found herself speechless. It was a shocking answer—in part because it was unexpected, but more so because it was the first time that Gabrielle had truly opened up that evening. "I can understand what you mean," she said. "For me, escape is getting away from it all. Going somewhere physically, leaving behind stresses and problems for another day."

The waiter finally brought their main courses, and Abby assumed the conversation would dry up again, but Gabrielle continued to smile at Abby. "Do you enjoy traveling then?"

Abby shrugged. "I've never really had the chance. Holidays back in Iowa to see my grandparents. We went skiing once when I was in college. But travel is expensive."

"Tell me your dream vacation."

Abby settled back, finishing her small appetizer and sipping her wine carefully. "How do you know that I have a dream vacation?"

Gabrielle met her gaze over her wine glass. "The way you speak," she said. "You crave escape just like I do. You long for adventure, and to see something incredible. And you are a reader, too. We share the same longing for escape and cling to books as a method of doing so. You are a librarian, which means you love books so much that you want to share those adventures with others. Am I wrong?"

The words took Abby's breath away. She'd known Gabrielle for only a short period, but already the other woman seemed to know her better than anyone else. "No," she said quietly. "You're not wrong."

"Then tell me," Gabrielle said.

chapter Seven

So Abby talked. She told Gabrielle about wanting to take a road trip across the United States. About wanting to see Rome and Moscow and Tokyo, and how books only barely sated the craving.

The entrée was a decadent lamb that melted on Abby's tongue, but she barely tasted the food. Instead, she found herself drawn into a conversation about literature, about places around the world that they'd both scene on television and in movies. Gabrielle turned that bright gaze on her, and Abby wasn't able to look away.

At some point, Gabrielle's foot slid along her own under the table. Abby moved her foot away, retreating to her own space.

Gabrielle followed. A soft leg pressed against her's, ankle to ankle, warm and strangely decadent under the long table cloth. Abby thought about moving her foot again, putting an end to the silent flirtation. But in the end she left it, her entire focus narrowing down to a spot of warmth on her leg.

"Do you write as well?" Gabrielle asked.

Abby shook her head. "I enjoy reading other people's stories, and making my own up, but putting words to the page has always escaped me. What about you? I bet you have an amazing story, even though you don't think so."

Gabrielle shook her head. "I have nothing interesting to tell."

Abby tried again. "What about the man from the gala Your manager, right?"

That was clearly the wrong topic to bring up. Gabrielle's eyes narrowed and her lips pressed together, anger rushing over before being chased by well-practiced blankness. "Yes," she said simply.

"I hope I didn't get you in trouble with him."

Gabrielle shook her head once. "Nothing for you to worry about," she said. "He will get what's coming to him eventually." She waved her hand dismissively. "I would rather talk about more pleasant things. Tell me about the library. What do you do there?"

But Gabrielle's change in mood had affected Abby as well, and she found herself remembering the conversation with Brian, the news article. "I might not be a librarian for much longer," she admitted.

"Why?" The question was oddly fierce, as though Gabrielle was truly desperate to know the answer.

Abby blinked up at her, surprised, and saw Gabrielle focused on her intently, brows furrowed. "They're talking about closing our branch down," she said. "Budget cuts. The city doesn't want to pay for libraries when they think they're pointless."

"But you love the library. You are passionate about your job the way—" Gabrielle sat back in her chair, biting her lip.

There was a moment of silence while Abby waited to see if Gabrielle would continue. Gabrielle's face was mostly blank, but there was something in her eyes, a hint of sadness that made Abby want to reach across the table to take her hand. But after a second even that tiny flicker of emotion vanished, and Gabrielle was once again calm and focused entirely on Abby.

"I don't have much of a say in it." Abby tried to keep her voice light. "I think it will do a lot of damage to the community if they close it. People rely on our services. It's not just checking out books . . . it's a place for people to meet up, to find information, to learn and explore."

Gabrielle seemed subdued and oddly vulnerable. "I truly hope that you do not lose your dream job." The words were spoken with an earnestness that only someone who had gone through something similar would feel. Except Gabrielle was still a famous model, and that was a dream job if Abby had ever heard of one.

"It is what it is." Abby took a deep breath, trying to tuck her own worry away where Gabrielle wouldn't see it. "Obviously I would prefer the branch not close, but at this point it's still just talk. At least, I hope."

That seemed to be the end of that conversation.

Abby tried to engage her in other topics. "I read that you were on Broadway for a while," she tried. She only got a nod. Another attempt: "I'm halfway through the biography of Alexander Hamilton;

my friend Nathan got tickets to see the play from his partner as an early birthday present, but I'll have to make do with the book." That warranted a brief, stilted discussion about the wildly popular play, but the conversation quickly dwindled again.

Whereas Gabrielle had been passionate about acting before, now it seemed like the topic was a closed one. Abby wanted to ask why she didn't act anymore, but the look on Gabrielle's face told her the question would be an unwelcome one.

It seemed like nothing Abby could talk about was of interest to Gabrielle. Suddenly Gabrielle appeared bored by Abby's attempts to connect. *Is this what an animal in a cage feels like, having someone curiously stare at them before moving on?* As though to solidify the thought, the touch on her ankle let up slowly, then vanished altogether.

"Thank you for dinner," Abby said finally, setting her fork down. It worked with her parents, a sign that she was ready to leave—and a less-than-subtle way to escape awkward family conversations. "I enjoyed the meal a lot. But I should probably get going before it gets too late."

Gabrielle appeared surprised by the sudden end to the meal. "I had thought you would want to enjoy dessert." Her head tilted to the side, those dark eyes focusing intently on Abby. "Perhaps at my apartment, rather than here?"

The mixed singles were sending Abby's brain into overdrive. It was like Gabrielle was running hot and cold, except it seemed more like cold and slightly tepid. But Abby wasn't so oblivious to think this invitation was anything other than a heated one.

"I can't. But thank you. This was . . . an interesting experience."

Gabrielle was watching her with a different expression now, one that Abby couldn't decipher. She didn't speak though. Instead, she held up her hand for the waiter, handed him a sleek credit card before he could even present her with the bill, and kept her eyes focused on Abby the entire time.

"I'm sorry," Abby said.

"For what?"

Gabrielle didn't seem upset, but her unreadable expression still made Abby nervous. "For . . . whatever you're thinking about me right now."

"I'm thinking," Gabrielle said, "that I have listened to your stories tonight, but I find that I am still surprised as I continue to learn more about you. Pleasantly surprised." Her mouth opened and she shifted, clearly about to add something else to that. Then she paused and closed her mouth.

Abby desperately wanted to know what Gabrielle had been about to say. She wanted to ask Gabrielle what she meant by "*pleasantly surprised*", but her dinner companion just looked away and finished her glass of wine off.

The waiter returned, and Gabrielle signed her name with a flourish before rising. "Allow me to walk you out at least.".

Abby rose, wobbling only slightly in her heels as the alcohol put her off-balance. "Sure," she said. "Thank you for dinner."

"Of course." Gabrielle twined their elbows together and led them from the restaurant. She helped Abby slide into her coat, hands deft and firm on Abby's shoulders and light on her neck as she straightened the collar. Goosebumps rose down Abby's arms and her skin tingled at the barely-there touches.

Gabrielle waited until the cab had pulled up, then stepped closer and brushed a soft kiss on Abby's cheek. Her hair brushed Abby's neck, and she smelled incredible, like vanilla and some kind of spice.

"It was a pleasure to have dinner with you tonight," she said into Abby's ear.

Her breath was warm on Abby's neck, and Abby shivered in the cool night air.

"Thank you again," she managed. "It was amazing."

Gabrielle stepped back and smiled. "Good night, Abigail."

It was only when Abby was in the cab and pulling away through the well-lit Manhattan streets that she realized that she had talked the entire meal, but hadn't learned a single thing about Gabrielle other than her love of reading. There had been a connection when Gabrielle had relaxed, a tentative thread between them in the rare moments when Gabrielle had opened up. The shared passion for books, the way she was so interested in Abby's dreams of traveling and the way Abby was in turn interested in uncovering more of who Gabrielle really was.

But there was still something bothering her. Abby watched the skyline as they drove over the bridge into Brooklyn, and tried to sort through her thoughts.

Gabrielle had clearly wanted to have sex at the end of the night. Had expected it, and been surprised when Abby dismissed her attempts to move the conversation in that direction. And the man who had interrupted them, Peter . . . Abby was pretty good at reading people, so while it was obvious he'd slept with Gabrielle before, she was fairly certain that Gabrielle wasn't interested in having sex with him again.

She remembered what Laura had said, about having sex without a relationship. Was that who Gabrielle was? Someone who just wanted to have sex? If so, it was a good thing Abby hadn't gotten too attached; they might have a few things in common, but there was no way they'd ever be compatible in that area.

chapter

Eight

Abby kicked her sore feet up on an empty chair and leaned back, rolling her shoulders and making a half-hearted grab for her bag. She managed to snag one of the handles and pull it closer. Digging through it produced a plastic bag tied up, the contents of which made her stomach growl as they were revealed: A sandwich, apple, can of Diet Coke, and half a chocolate bar.

It was nothing on the elegant meal from last night. But then her feet hadn't yet recovered from another night in heels, and at least she could pronounce "ham sandwich" without sounding like an idiot.

Saturdays at the library were always busy; she usually worked Monday to Friday, but filling in on weekends when someone took a day off was common enough. Abby settled back into her chair, digging into her lunch, and dug her phone out of her bag. Sometimes she had a chance to check it during the day, but the only person who ever messaged her during work was her mother. Today, however, Abby hadn't had a chance yet to even glance at her phone, and was surprised to see several missed calls and texts. Most of them were from Sara of all people, and Abby sipped on her soda while tapping through the messages.

SARA: *girl you need to answer your phone.*

SARA: *ok obvs you haven't seen the news yet or you'd be callin me*

NATHAN: *Sara says you're internet-famous now?*

SARA: *youre prob at work according to nate so here click this when you go on break.*

There was a link in the last text, and Abby stared at the conversation in confusion before hovering her finger over the website. It was one of those shortened links, so she couldn't even begin to guess what it was about, except that apparently she was on the internet?

Curiosity won over caution, and she tapped the screen, watching in growing shock as the page loaded.

Model Gabrielle Levesque spotted at Printemps with unknown female companion.

The article had a clear picture of Gabrielle, looking over Abby's bare shoulder. Abby had turned her head slightly, but only a small part of her face was visible. The article went on to speculate about who the mysterious woman was, if it had been a date, and if The Ice Queen was actually a lesbian.

It was vicious and unsparing. It was a gross invasion of privacy.

Abby set her sandwich aside, suddenly no longer hungry.

Voices carried into the break room, and Abby closed out of the page on her phone, feeling guilty and humiliated. Brian walked in with Marcy, the supervisor of the library. They were talking quietly, but both stopped and stared at Abby when they walked in.

Do they know?

Abby looked away, fidgeting.

"Guess you saw the article then," Marcy said dryly.

Oh. Shit. "Yeah," Abby said meekly.

"There's gonna be trouble." Marcy was older, a New York native who was known in the library community as being tough to work for, and who rarely showed emotion. It made her impossible to read, and Abby was never sure if she was in a bad mood or not. But she mostly left Abby, Brian, and the rest of the staff alone to do their jobs. Today though, her heavy New York accent was even thicker, and she looked weary.

"Trouble?" Abby looked up, afraid. Was she going to be in trouble for dating someone? Because she went out with a woman? She'd never thought Marcy or Brian were homophobes.

Brian nodded grimly. "You should probably start giving some thought to finding a position at another branch."

This can't be happening. Abby clenched her fists, resting them on her knees to keep them steady. "How much trouble am I in?"

"We're *all* in trouble," Marcy said. "They're giving us until June 15."

Wait, what? "What?"

Brian swung a chair around and sat down. "I think even when I saw that article with the proposed list of library closures, I thought 'it won't really happen'. But I guess I was wrong. The article in today's paper confirms it."

The article? Abby blinked, shoulders dropping. "They're really closing the library?" Her entire body sagged, a combination of relief—*they don't know about my dinner date with Gabrielle*—and dismay.

Marcy studied her for a minute, apparently weighing Abby's reaction, before nodding. "Seems like," she said. "The NYPL is looking at closing three or four branches, and BPL another two. Queens is still deciding. We're on the cutting block."

Abby closed her eyes.

"It's not set in stone yet," Brian added.

"Don't get your hopes up."

Abby opened her eyes to find Brian frowning at Marcy. "People have managed to save libraries from closure before," he said. "And there's still one more City Council meeting in mid-May."

"They've already made their decision." Marcy crossed her arms, and her words were flat. "Best we can do is accept it and move on."

Abby fixed her eyes on her phone and thought about the expensive cab rides the night before, the fancy dinner and life of luxury that she'd briefly glimpsed at. Then she thought about her meager savings, and the bleak job search ahead of her. She and Gabrielle were two very different women, living in two very different worlds.

"I should probably get back to work," she said with a sigh.

"Why?" Brian quirked a humorless grin. "Library's closing, we might as well slack off and kick our feet up, right?"

Marcy shot him a glare that threatened severe pain. "I think someone needs to go shelve and reorganize the children's section for a few hours."

Brian's eyes widened. "It was a joke, Mars. I was *joking*."

"I'm not. Shoo." She made a sweeping gesture with her fingers, and sent Brian out into the library. Once he was gone she turned back to Abby. "Something's bothering you," she said. "Could tell when we walked in. And it isn't the closure . . ."

Abby's shoulders jerked in a half-hearted shrug. "It's fine. Just personal stuff."

"Boy problems?"

"Something like that."

"My advice? Figure out a way to get rid of the personal crap. Life's about to get a hell of a lot more stressful. Best to cut the other stress when you can."

Abby gave her a thin smile. "Yeah, I suspect you're right," she said. "Thanks Marcy. I'll be up at the desk in a few minutes."

Marcy waved her off. "We interrupted your lunch," she said. "Take a few minutes to finish your food."

It was an uncharacteristic display of generosity, and one that Abby wasn't about to say no to. She nodded. "Thanks, will do."

Marcy headed back out to the front, and Abby stared at her phone like it was a poisonous snake before carefully unlocking it and pulling the news story up once again. She stared at the picture, part of her face and Gabrielle's own carefully postured body. Gabrielle seemed . . . not cold. She wasn't the Ice Queen that the news kept calling her, not from what Abby had seen. But indifferent maybe. Distant. A remote island that Abby had no hope of reaching.

She closed out of the article and began drafting a reply to Sara and Nathan. From the texts before, Abby got the impression that they were both excited about the article—that neither of them saw it as the awful invasion that Abby did. They thought it was cool that Abby was "internet famous". Abby exhaled as she typed out a response. *Saw the article. Good picture. Meal was tasty, company was interesting. One-time thing, so I guess that's my five seconds of anonymous fame.*

Sara responded with a wink and a *hope you had a good time after dinner.*

Abby remembered the surprise on Gabrielle's face when she'd turned down the offer of dessert.

Just another reason among many why they wouldn't work out.

With a definitive click, she turned her phone off and stuck it back in her bag. It had been one night, a chance to peek her head into another world for a few hours, and dinner with a beautiful woman. A once-in-a-lifetime experience..

And if she couldn't get Gabrielle's intense dark eyes out of her head? Well, it's not like the dream could hurt anything.

The next week dragged on. Nothing changed at work, even though everything had changed. Brian and Marcy seemed to be walking on eggshells, and the other employees weren't any better off. Abby kept her head down and focused on work; there were still events and story times to schedule, books to check in and out, and a library to keep running.

A few patrons came up to talk to her about the library closing. Some were accepting, others passionately opposed. Abby listened to all of them, nodding and agreeing.

She broke the news to Jenna at the end of the week, when it became clear that no miracle phone call was going to come about keeping their branch open. Her roommate wasn't happy.

"Our lease isn't up until September," Jenna said.

"I know."

Jenna leaned forward. "Can't you just transfer to another branch?"

Abby thought about trying to explain. There were too few job openings as is—add in the branches closing, and things got much tighter. "I have a few possibilities," she said instead. "And I have enough in savings to be okay for a while."

"Damn. I hope you can find something soon. I know you love working at the library." Jenna sighed. "But if you can't pay your half of the rent, you gotta give me as much notice as you can."

"I will."

They'd always gotten along, but neither of them made enough money to shoulder the rent alone. The realization that Abby might not be able to afford her portion was clearly worrying Jenna.

"It'll be okay," Abby said. She didn't believe the words, but they seemed to help reassure Jenna. "Ideally I won't be out of work at all, and can start at a new branch as soon as this one closes."

Jenna nodded. "Alright. Just let me know."

"I will."

They sat together for a moment, the TV a low wash of white noise in the background. Then Jenna straightened.

"What's with the fancy dress and heals that I spotted in your room?" she asked. "You went on a date? Wearing heels? I didn't even know you owned clothes like that!"

Abby flushed. She'd managed to keep Gabrielle out of her thoughts over the last few days by a combination of more important things to worry over and sheer will-power. But she did still have Sara's dress and shoes hanging up on her door. "I borrowed them," she explained. "It wasn't a date though. Just a nice dinner with a friend."

"Some friend. You don't dress up like that unless you're planning to get some after."

Abby shifted. "Nothing happened after."

"Your words say one thing, but that blush on your face says another," Jenna teased.

Why was everyone so obsessed with Abby having sex with someone? "Nothing happened. Just dinner. Not a date."

There was a knock at the door.

Jenna gave Abby a long look, then stood and went to the door. She talked with someone for a minute, then came back into the living room with her hands full.

"Not a date, huh?" she asked.

Abby's eyes widened as she took in what Jenna was carrying: roses. A dozen of them, long stem, the same stunning red as the dress Gabrielle had been wearing the first time Abby had seen her.

It had been days since the dinner, and Abby had assumed that Gabrielle had forgotten about her the same way that Abby was trying to forget about Gabrielle. But an expensive bouquet of flowers was the exact opposite of forgetting.

But it was more of the same from Gabrielle: hot and cold, back and forth. They'd had a connection while dancing, and then Gabrielle hadn't called for several days. Conversation over dinner had been a mess of tension and awkward silences, interspersed with rare signs of emotion from Gabrielle. And now another long silence, followed by a very obvious show of passion.

"Oh."

"That's all you've got?" Jenna carefully deposited the vase on the table, and Abby could immediately smell the sweet floral scent.

"It . . . It wasn't a date."

Jenna plucked the card from the flowers and handed it over. "I think your dinner companion thinks differently."

Abby's fingers felt numb as she opened the envelope and slid the small piece of stock paper out. The note was hand-written, a flowing cursive that took a second to decipher.

"Thank you for the very enjoyable night," she read out loud. "Perhaps we can have dinner again soon . . . this time with . . ."

"This time with what?" Jenna prompted. She was clearly fascinated, staring wide-eyed as though seeing Abby for the first time.

Abby blushed. "This time with dessert."

Jenna grinned. "Told you. Definitely a date. You gonna go out with him again?"

"I don't know." Abby frowned, processing Jenna's question. Jenna had assumed it was a man, just like everyone else. Jenna had assumed that they were going to have sex too, just like everyone else.

Too many assumptions. What was Gabrielle assuming?

"Probably not," Abby amended.

Jenna frowned, disappointed, but didn't push. "Fair enough. At least you got some nice flowers out of it. One nice thing after the bad news about your work."

"Yeah." Abby stared at the flowers, remembering fiery eyes and that stunning dress. "One nice thing."

chapter

Nine

Nathan had his feet kicked up on Sara's coffee table when Abby walked in.

"The door was open," she said.

"Because I'm too tired to get back up, and Sara said you were coming over."

Abby hung her coat up and nudged the door shut behind her. "You're gonna get robbed."

Nathan shrugged her off. "Sara's tough, she'll fight anyone who tries to rob us."

"Us?" Sara came out of the kitchen with two cups of wine. "You don't live here anymore, rich boy." She handed the second glass to Abby with a wink, who took it gratefully.

Nathan stuck out his lower lip. "Mean. And you didn't bring me anything to drink?"

Sara took a long sip from her own glass. "The last time you were here you told me you'd replace the bottle you drank. Since you didn't bring one, no more of my wine for you."

Abby sat back, laughing, and took a sip of the cheap wine that was both awful and comfortably familiar at the same time. *They bicker like brother and sister.* Nathan's lip was jutting out, and Sara watching him with obvious fondness behind her berating. *And Sara would totally be the 'big sister' in their relationship.* To Abby, who was an only child, it was fascinating to watch them together. That they included her so easily in their friendship was incredible.

"I ordered the Chinese," Nathan protested. "Do I get wine for putting food on the table tonight?"

Sara turned to Abby, eyes laughing even though she was clearly trying desperately to keep a straight face. "What do you think, Abs?"

"Well," Abby pondered. "He does work very hard."

"So hard," Nathan agreed, pouting beneath wide blue eyes.

"And he *did* buy us dinner."

Nathan nodded eagerly.

Sara laughed out loud. "Fine. You can bring a bottle with you the next time you come over.".

Abby took another sip. *What I wouldn't give to have a relationship like that. Someday, hopefully.* "So, to what do I owe the dinner invite? You give me alcohol, promise me greasy delivery for dinner . . . there must be a catch."

Nathan heaved himself off the couch with a long-suffering sigh, raising his voice as he trudged into the kitchen. "We wanted to know about your date," he called.

Sara took over. "It's been two weeks. You texted that you were going to stop by to return the dress and shoes, so I figured we'd bribe you with food in exchange for all the juicy details."

"Please tell me there are juicy details," Nathan said, returning to the room with his own glass and collapsing onto the couch. "Jason's been busy the last week because of some huge reorganization project, so I need to live vicariously through someone else's relationship."

Sara eyed him. "That's more than I needed to know about *your* relationship."

"Liar," Nathan snarked back, grinning. He turned his full attention on Abby. "We're both terribly nosey friends. Tell us everything."

Abby shifted uncomfortably. "There's nothing to tell."

Sara leaned forward. "But you went to dinner with a celebrity. You were on a gossip news site. At the very least tell us about her. Is she as frigid as everyone says?"

This, thankfully, was more stable ground for Abby. "We had dinner. It was alternatively awkward and lovely." Her first instinct was to defend Gabrielle, to tell Sara and Nathan about her small smiles and the way her eyes burned when she met Abby's. But then she remembered the rest of the night and hesitated. The posture that never seemed to relax, the way she avoided talking about herself, the impossible distance between them.

"She's emotionally detached," Abby said after a moment. "I've never met anyone who runs so hot and cold like she does. She's not the cruel Ice Queen that everyone says, but I couldn't figure out why she would—" She bit her lip.

Sara's eyes lit up. "Why she would what?"

Abby mumbled into her wine glass.

"Abs," Nathan said.

Abby sighed. "She sent me roses. After the date. A dozen long stem red roses."

Nathan let out a low whistle, and Sara gave Abby an appraising look. "Guess that answers how the sex was then," she said.

"There was no sex!" The words escaped Abby before she could stop herself.

Sara's eyebrows furrowed in confusion. "Then what *did* happen? In my experience, you don't get red roses like that after a first date unless the night ended *really* well, or unless you're hoping for a second date."

Abby shrugged. "Nothing happened," she said. "I said goodnight, got in a cab, went home. There was almost no connection. Nothing."

Nathan tilted his head to the side. "You don't want to have sex with her."

Abby frowned while Sara turned to stare at him, clearly waiting for him to explain his words. Nathan was good at reading people—better than Abby herself was—and at knowing what they were thinking. It was how he'd first gotten the attention of his partner, by studying Jason and learning about him. Abby wasn't surprised he'd figured her out too.

"No," she said finally.

Sara turned to study Abby instead. "I thought you were into women."

"I am." Abby struggled with the words. "I'm into women, and men sometimes too. I like dating. I just . . . don't like sex."

The words sat heavily in the room for a long moment. The tension was broken by the buzzer, and the sound cut through the awkward silence as Sara quickly rose to let the delivery guy in.

When she returned a minute later, bags of food over each wrist and a heavenly smell filling the room, she seemed to have come to a conclusion. "So, you're like saving yourself for marriage?"

Nathan opened his mouth, then closed it, watching Abby carefully. He nodded at her, a silent show of support, and sat back to wait for her to respond.

"No. And it's not a religious thing either," Abby finally said. She accepted the carton of chow mein when it was handed to her, but didn't open it.

"Then what is it?"

Abby fiddled with the food in her hands, letting the warmth seep into her palms and comfort her. "Have you ever heard of asexuality?"

Sara shook her head, but Nathan was nodding now, understanding quickly filling his face. "You're ace."

"Yeah." Abby shrugged. "I don't really talk about it. It's . . . not easy, you know?" She kept her eyes on her food and pressed her lips closed.

Sara was still struggling to grasp it, and the way she was frowning and biting her lip made Abby shift uncomfortably. Nathan picked up his own food and, when it was obvious Abby wasn't going to respond, came to her rescue. "She doesn't experience sexual attraction to people. Like, that's her orientation. I'm homosexual, and I'm sexually attracted to other men. You're heterosexual and are sexually attracted to the opposite gender. And Abby is asexual, so she's sexually attracted to no one."

Abby peered up tentatively, finding Nathan smiling at her, eyes full of acceptance. Sara was still visibly confused, glancing back and forth between Nathan and Abby as she opened her mouth and closed it again, but she didn't look upset. "Yeah, what he said."

Sara nodded slowly. "Okay, I can respect that," she said. "I mean, I don't get it personally, but I can't judge or anything."

Abby met her gaze and smiled tentatively. "I thought you might be angry."

That got a startled look from Sara. "Angry? Why would I have any right to be upset about who you do or don't want to sleep with?"

"Most people don't understand. Like, they think there's something wrong with it. I've heard it all: That it's not natural, or that I haven't found the right person. Some people call asexuals 'robots', or think we've been sexually abused in the past. I've found it easier to just not talk about it."

Sara stabbed a piece of beef viciously. "Well screw them, then. Nothing wrong with you doing whatever you want or don't want with your own body."

Abby smiled slightly, relaxing enough to finally release her grip on her food and open the carton. Nathan and Sara's easy acceptance was a huge relief. "Gabrielle invited me to her apartment after dinner. She seemed surprised when I said no."

Nathan frowned. "Don't let her pressure you. If you do go out again."

"I'm a big girl, Nate," Abby said, rolling her eyes even as she smiled. "I can take care of myself."

But Sara was nodding in agreement. "Just because she's famous and sends you flowers doesn't mean you have to say yes to a second date."

"There's not going to be a second date," Abby insisted.

Sara gave her a look. "She sent you red roses. I bet you a bottle of wine that costs more than twenty bucks that she'll call you any day now."

Abby's phone rang halfway through Monday afternoon. She'd tucked it into her pocket instead of leaving it in her bag, and it vibrated against her leg as she helping a young man locate a graphic novel series. She found the book, motioned for Brian to help him check out, and slipped in the back to check the call.

She'd been hoping it was a library a little further south that was calling her back. The number on the screen, however, had a name attached to it.

"Dammit," Abby muttered. She owed Sara a bottle of wine. Maybe she could steal that from her parents' house as well . . . hopefully she could get in and out while they weren't home, and avoid the awkward conversation that was sure to come up when her mother asked her how work was going.

There was no voicemail this time. Abby hesitated, thinking about what Sara and Nathan had said. If she called back, was it because she felt pressured into another date?

But Gabrielle hadn't pressured her that night. Abby had said no to dessert—and likely to something more—and Gabrielle had backed off immediately.

Abby exhaled and called her back.

"Gabrielle Levesque's phone." It was a brusque man's voice that answered, not the smooth voice with a hint of French accent that was quickly becoming familiar.

"Oh." Abby hesitated. "I'm . . . is Gabrielle there?"

The man's voice grew deeper. "Who is this?"

There was the sound of a scruffle, and then Gabrielle's voice in the background, clearly upset. Abby couldn't make out the words at first, but then Gabrielle must have gotten ahold of the phone. "Don't answer my calls. And go away." She bit out the words, holding the phone away from her mouth but still close enough that Abby could hear the ice in every syllable. There was a muted reply, and then Gabrielle was speaking to Abby. "Abigail, I did not expect you to return my call right away."

Abby gripped the phone to her ear. "It's quiet at work today." *Hot and cold for sure.* Gabrielle had gone from frigid rage to gentle warmth in a split second. "I had a second."

Gabrielle's voice softened further. "I am glad that you called. Did you receive the flowers I sent?"

"Yeah. They're gorgeous."

"I'm glad you enjoy them." Gabrielle did seem pleased by this. "I do apologize for sending them to your home, though you did not give me your address. When your friend registered your name at the charity gala, he also included your contact information."

Oh, Abby hadn't even thought of that. She bit her lip. Was she supposed to feel flattered, or creeped out?

"It crossed a line, and I apologize," Gabrielle said, before Abby could make up her mind.

"It's okay." Gabrielle clearly had connections, if she'd been able to wheedle Abby's address out of the event planner.

Gabrielle hummed lightly. "I would like to see you again, Abigail." She spoke slowly, like she was thinking over each word, but the effect was less tentative and more precise. "But I do not think a public meal so soon after our last one would be in our best interests."

"You saw the gossip news site?" Abby asked.

"Unfortunately, yes." Gabrielle was obviously displeased. "I apologize for yet another intrusion into your privacy."

"It's okay," Abby repeated, though the memory of the article was enough to send a chill down her spine. "But yeah, I don't know that I want to repeat that."

"May I offer an alternative then?" Gabrielle didn't wait for a response. "Have dinner with me in my apartment. I can have a meal catered, and perhaps we can watch a movie or simply talk. I am curious to learn more about you."

Gabrielle's apartment? Abby hesitated.

"*Don't let her pressure you,*" Nathan had said.

"I'm not sure."

Gabrielle quickly picked up on her reluctance. "Only dinner and a movie," she said, "in the comfort and privacy of my apartment." She paused, and then her voice warmed. "I would very much like to see you again, Abigail."

It was the warmth that convinced Abby. "Alright. Dinner and a movie sounds good."

She couldn't see Gabrielle's smile, but she could hear it in her response. "Excellent. I must run, Abigail, but I look forward to seeing you soon."

c h a p t e r

Ten

Three things happened in the days between Gabrielle's phone call and the date.

The first was that Abby had brunch with her parents.

Her mother called her the evening after she spoke with Gabrielle, while she was making dinner around Jenna, both of them trying to use the tiny kitchen at the same time. Abby ceded the stove to Jenna when her phone rang, wiping her hands on a towel and grabbing the phone without looking at the display.

"Why didn't you tell me about the library?"

Abby pulled the phone away from her ear, glanced up at the ceiling, counted to ten, and then brought the phone back. "Hi mom," she said. "How are you? Did you and dad get to that antiques market you were talking about visiting?"

Jenna gave her a wide-eyed stare that clearly said *better you than me.*

Abby motioned for her to turn off the stove under Abby's dinner, then escaped down the hall to her room, nudging the door shut behind her. Knowing her mom, this was going to be a long one.

"I talked to you two days ago," her mother said. "Why didn't you mention that your library was closing then?"

"Because I didn't want to have this conversation." Abby's brain-to-mouth filter was apparently defective. She regretted the words a split second later when her mother took a deep breath and began to talk.

Which was how, on her day off that week, she found herself hopping the LIRR out to a restaurant near her parents' house for brunch and sipping weak mimosas while her mother went on at length about how useless Abby's Masters was and her father drank black coffee and exchanged occasional sympathetic smiles with his daughter.

"Mom," Abby finally said, setting her fork down next to her omelet. "It's fine. There's still a chance the library won't close, but if it does I'm working on finding another branch to transfer to."

"Why don't you get your teaching certification?" It was a question she'd asked a dozen times before, and the answer had never changed no matter how many times Abby had responded.

"I have no interest in teaching. I *like* working at the library."

She contemplated her mimosa while her mother went off on another tirade, wondering if there was enough champagne in the world to help her get through the meal.

But survive it she did, her mother eventually winding down. By Abby's count, there had only been four *I told you so*'s, so she counted it as a win and carried her bone-weary body back home.

The second thing that happened was that she opened the New York Times' Arts section on her work computer Wednesday morning to check out the latest book reviews, and proceeded to spill hot coffee across her desk when Gabrielle's face appeared front and center on her monitor.

She ignored Brian's snort of laughter and quickly mopped up the spill before it could get all over her keyboard and papers. By the time her desk was clean, there were patrons waiting to ask her questions, and she had to minimize the page and hide Gabrielle's model-perfect smile away until it was time to take a break.

It was mid-morning before she found five minutes to pull the site back up. What she'd half-expected to be a headline hallucinated from a lack of caffeine was most definitely real: *Gabrielle Levesque from backstage to runway.*

It was an interview with Gabrielle about an upcoming fashion show that she was closing. Abby gathered from the opening paragraph that it was a huge step for her, and that the closing model was a high honor to be given. She greedily devoured the article, hoping for some insight into the woman she knew so little about.

But Gabrielle seemed purposefully vague. She deflected most personal questions, answered those she couldn't brush off with only the barest hint of an answer. The interviewer noted that she was "a woman of few words" and "distant", which had Abby frowning.

Why was Gabrielle so cold to the rest of the world?

Toward the end of the article, though, the interviewer seemed surprised when he asked a question about Gabrielle's backstage preparations before her shows.

"Levesque comes alive when she discusses what she's currently reading in the makeup chair," the article said, "talking animatedly about a science fiction novel that she was recommended by a good friend. 'It's rare for me to meet people who understand my love of books,' Levesque explains. 'Reading is an escape and a method of relaxation, and I am lucky to have met someone with whom I can share that.'"

The article wound its way back to the information about the runway show, but Abby only skimmed the last few words, her mind back on the previous paragraph. The interview had only been put up on the Times website that morning, and it had been more than two weeks since they'd had dinner and talked about books over foie gras and lamb.

Gabrielle had remembered her book recommendation. For some reason, seeing the evidence of that on her computer screen in plain black text had Abby actually looking forward to their next date.

And the third thing that happened was that Abby once again found herself begging for Sara's assistance to pick out an outfit. This time, though, she found both Nathan and Sara on her doorstep. Jenna watched in amusement from the couch while the three of them headed down the hall to Abby's tiny bedroom, clothes and makeup in hand.

"Here," Nathan said, passing her two hangers that he'd had draped over his arm. "I didn't know that I was agreeing to be a pack mule when I said I wanted in on the secret makeover session."

Sara rolled her eyes at him.

Abby held up the clothing, surprised to see that there were no sexy little dresses for her to try on. Instead there was a lovely sweater in a creamy color, the knit light-weight and soft to the touch instead of itchy. A dark gray skirt went with it.

"Fashionable for a date," Sara explained, "without screaming *sex* like the tiny dresses she's seen you in before. More comfortable."

Abby blinked up at her, surprised. "Thank you," she said, hoping Sara could see the gratitude in her eyes.

"You like her." Nathan slouched against the wall. "You're nervous about the date tonight, which you wouldn't be if you didn't actually *like* her."

Abby shrugged awkwardly. "She's fascinating. And beautiful. I want to know all about her. I want to know what her story is."

"You can read her story on Wikipedia," Nathan said.

Sara motioned for him to turn around, which he did with an eye roll. "Get changed while you chat," she said to Abby. "We don't have much time."

"That's not her story," Abby said. "That's a bunch of pieces of information compiled by strangers. They don't tell me who she is. They don't tell me why the rest of the world calls her the Ice Queen when I see the fire beneath the surface."

Nathan let out a long sigh, still patiently looking at the wall while Abby blushingly stripped down in front of Sara to pull on the clothes. "I'm torn here," he said. "I've heard so many stories from so many different people. On the one hand, you clearly like her, and I want you to be happy. But on the other hand, I want to warn you, because I know you're going to get your heart broken by her. Levesque's reputation is *not* a good one, Abs."

"But you won't," Sara cut in. "It's Abby's choice. And obviously there's more to her than what the rumors say, if Abby's seeing it."

Abby tugged the sleeves of the sweater down over her hands, suddenly chilled. "I just want to figure her out for myself," she said. "Other people's stories are great, but the stories I can find myself are almost always better."

Sara hummed in approval, but her gaze was on the outfit Abby was wearing, and she didn't seem to be focusing on Abby's words. "You look sexy as hell, lady."

"Can I turn around now?" Nathan didn't wait for an answer and peered over his shoulder. He grinned and turned the rest of the way around. "I mean, I know nothing about fashion, but you look gorgeous."

"Hair and make-up, quickly. Then you need to get into the city." Sara motioned for Abby to sit.

"I wish I didn't need to do this every time," Abby said softly, letting Sara guide her to the bed. Nathan obligingly held out Sara's shoebox of makeup; it wasn't as impressive as Laura's giant cases had been, but the contents were just as varied and overflowing.

"You're going on a date," Sara pointed out. "Girls dress up on dates. It's a thing."

Abby bit her lip but didn't move as Sara descended with brushes and foundation. "It feels like a lie. This isn't me. I'm not a girl who gets dressed up and puts on make-up to go out. If it was up to me I'd be wearing a nice pair of jeans and maybe a blouse?"

Nathan watched her silently.

"How can I go on a date with someone that I'm tricking?" Abby asked.

Sara seemed to be focused on smoothing concealer evenly and didn't respond, so Nathan answered instead. "I'm probably not the best person to talk about being honest with the person you're seeing." He'd spent more than six months lying to his partner Jason before finally coming clean, and the revelation had torn their relationship apart before Nathan had painstakingly stitched it back together. "But I think this is just adding a shine to someone who's already beautiful inside and out."

"Cheesy," Sara said, "but true."

"Wearing nice clothes and getting Sara to do your makeup doesn't change who you are. You and Gabrielle are still strangers, so you're kind of..." He paused. "You're making a good first impression, I guess. People tend judge each other on appearance before learning about who that person really is."

It made sense, and some of Abby's unease drained away. "Like rebinding a book," she said. "You can put a nice cover on it and convince someone to pick it up. But that doesn't change the contents... it's still the words inside that draw them in."

"You're such a nerd," Sara said fondly.

Abby grinned. "Thanks, Nate," she said. "Thank both of you. I'm pretty sure I'd be hiding at home with my phone off to avoid calls right now if I didn't have you to reassure me."

"That's what extroverted friends are for," Sara said. "To help draw introverts like you out of your shell for a few hours so you can enjoy new experiences. Now hold still while I put this eyeliner on."

Abby settled onto her bed. Tonight she'd get to talk to Gabrielle, see if she had a story worth hearing. And she'd get to tell more of her own story, and help Gabrielle see the real her beneath the fancy clothes and make-up.

By the time Sara and Nathan had finished their work, it was later than Abby had thought. She slipped on her own comfortable pair of flats, waved goodbye to her friends, and gathered her purse as she flew out the door. And with a grimace at the thought of spending more money unnecessarily, she held out her hand and flagged down a cab to take her into Manhattan.

chapter

Abby checked the address on her phone against the one on the building for the second time. Gabrielle had texted her address to Abby the day before, but Abby hadn't thought much about it until the cab driver had delivered her to the front of a gorgeous modern high-rise and departed with a staggering amount of Abby's hard-earned money.

A doorman let Abby in, and the clack of her shoes echoed in the marble-lined lobby as she found the elevator and hit the button for the fifth floor. The elevator ride was silent and quick, opening to reveal plush carpet and a quietly expensive hallway.

The text had said #501, so Abby wandered to the end of the hall and hesitated in front of the plain door for a moment. Gabrielle clearly lived in luxury, but it was the understated elegance of the building that had Abby's hands clenching into nervous fists.

She knocked before she could talk herself out of it.

Gabrielle answered the door, and Abby was suddenly too stunned to remember to be nervous.

"Abigail." Gabrielle gave her a small smile, but her eyes were heated as they raked over Abby from head to foot before returning to meet her gaze. "I'm so glad you could make it. Please, come in."

Abby tried not to stare too hard as she walked in. A short hallway led to a massive open sitting room and kitchen, all chrome and dark marble; the apartment was so big that Abby's own shared housing could fit inside with room to spare. But the most eye-catching feature was Gabrielle herself, wearing a lacy red blouse that revealed hints of tantalizing tanned skin and black jeans so tight that her legs seemed to go on for miles.

"You look beautiful," Gabrielle said, turning to give Abby another smile.

"Me?" Abby blinked. "You look . . . incredible. Gorgeous. I feel so plain in comparison."

Gabrielle frowned. "I wish I could show you what I am seeing. But I think even a mirror will only show you what you want to see about yourself. So I hope you will trust my words at least when I say that you are radiant."

Abby flushed and glanced away.

When she turned back, Gabrielle was still watching her with a strange intensity. "You are not what I expected," she said quietly, as though speaking to herself. She shifted, and suddenly the Gabrielle from the restaurant was back, polite smile in place. "We should eat before the food gets cold. I hope you enjoy Ethiopian?"

"I've never had it," Abby said honestly. She followed Gabrielle and the scent of spiced meat to the small table next to the kitchen area. Gabrielle had set out plates and glasses, and there were platters between them with enough food to feed half a dozen people.

"I wasn't sure what you might like, so I chose a variety of options. This is *injera*," she pointed to a spongy bread that was rolled up neatly on a plate, "and you use it as a spoon of sorts to pick up the other foods. Do you eat meat?"

"Sure," Abby said. "It smells heavenly."

"The flavors are incredible," Gabrielle agreed. She pulled out a chair for Abby. "Please sit."

The meal was surprisingly pleasant. Abby had expected stilted conversation similar to their first date at Printemps, with Gabrielle alternating between icy and warm. But she seemed more comfortable in her own home, smiling and talking easily as she explained *kik alicha* and *doro wat*.

"Have you been to Ethiopia?" Abby asked as she refilled her glass of wine.

"No. Perhaps someday." Gabrielle turned her focus on her plate.

Another dead end. She tried again. "Is this your favorite cuisine? It's so good, I could probably eat it all the time given the chance!"

Gabrielle seemed to think about this question. "It is a food associated with good memories for me," she said. "My mother's family was from Ethiopia, and she made food like this when I was little. My father, he did not approve of cuisine like this, so she would only make it when he was not at home."

It was the most Abby had learned about Gabrielle so far. "Is your mother a good cook?"

"She was." Gabrielle exhaled. "She passed away many years ago."

Gabrielle didn't seem upset, but Abby felt terrible. "I'm sorry," she said. "Does your father still live in Canada then?"

But Gabrielle was clearly done talking about her own life for the time being. She shrugged off the question and asked Abby to pass the *injera* instead. "What kind of movies do you enjoy?" she asked, managing to look prim and elegant while using her fingers to scoop up the food on her plate.

"Um, just about anything," Abby said. "Do you have a movie in mind?"

Gabrielle hummed. "A photographer that I work with often suggested a film. It has won several awards, so I thought we might try that." She gave the movie's title, but it was in Italian or Spanish so Abby just nodded and took another sip of her wine.

Abby waited to see if Gabrielle would continue speaking, maybe tell her about the movie or talk about her job. But as awkwardness again descended on the table, and Abby began to regret coming here for a second date. It was clear that while she and Gabrielle had some things in common, Gabrielle's reluctance to talk about herself was going to put a halt on any chance for them to get to know each other.

For the next few minutes, the only sound in the room was the scraping of plates. Abby thought about half a dozen questions, but dismissed each of them. *She'll only close off more if I ask her about herself, and she doesn't seem to care for small talk.*

Eventually they both sat back in their seats, wiping their hands clean. In silent agreement, they boxed up the rest of the food and Gabrielle led the way to a comfortable couch set in front of a large screen TV. A few buttons on the remote, and the menu for the film was queued up.

At least we won't have to talk, Abby thought. Gabrielle settled down on one side of the couch, and Abby took the other.

Thirty minutes in, Abby was wishing for the stilted conversation again instead of the subtitled movie. She looked over at Gabrielle, ready to ask where the restroom was in an attempt to escape the room for a few minutes, but—

Gabrielle was yawning, but attempting to hide the gesture behind her hand. *She's bored.* Abby watched as Gabrielle blinked, trying to focus on the screen. *More than bored.*

Abby threw caution to the wind, finding a thread of bravery and grabbing ahold of it. "Okay, I'm sorry, but this movie is terrible," she said. "Your photographer friend is pretentious and gives awful recommendations."

Gabrielle eyes widened as she turned to stare at Abby. For a second Abby thought she was offended. But then Gabrielle laughed.

Actually laughed.

The sound surprised Abby, but it was infectious and soon she was laughing too. "I'm sorry," she said. "I didn't mean to be so abrupt but I saw you yawning and realized that we're both watching this horrible movie for no good reason."

Gabrielle appeared younger when she relaxed, her eyes shining and bright and her entire body moving more easily. "You're right," she said. "And it's me who should apologize for suggesting such a poor film." She pushed off the couch and walked over to a cabinet beneath the TV. "Please come select something better. Your choice."

Still laughing, Abby followed her over, kneeling down until she was side-by-side with Gabrielle in front of the shelves. She could feel Gabrielle as a line of heat beside her, distracting and soft where their arms brushed together.

"Oh!" Abby ran a finger over one of the box sets. "You have the entire series?" She would recognize the spines of the Harry Potter movies anywhere, identical to her own much-watched set at home.

"Of course," Gabrielle said. "A small indulgence. I enjoy the story, a boy escaping from a terrible family and battling a great evil. It is something that I—" She closed her mouth with an audible click.

Abby was careful with her response. "I like the magic, and the way the bookworm saves the day over and over again."

"Ah. You're Hermione then."

Gabrielle was staring at her, so Abby met her gaze. "And you're Harry?"

A flicker of emotion passed through Gabrielle's eyes, there and gone in a heartbeat. "No," she said, turning back to the movies. "I'm afraid that I am not Gryffindor enough to be like Harry Potter."

Something in her voice made Abby's heart ache. She reached out, running her hand down Gabrielle's arm. "Let's watch something else then."

Gabrielle shuddered at the contact, but nodded. "Yes, I don't know that I can handle wizards and the battle of good versus evil tonight."

They decided on a classic Bond movie, and this time Abby settled on the couch closer to Gabrielle, sharing her own warmth in silent comfort.

Halfway through the movie, Abby felt eyes on her and turned to see Gabrielle looking at her again, instead of the screen.

"What?" she asked.

Gabrielle gave a small smile. "You are so beautiful when you're interested in something."

Heat rose on Abby's neck. "I'm nothing special."

"Abigail," Gabrielle said quietly, "you are so unique. Unlike anyone I have ever met before. You have no idea, do you?"

And then she leaned forward and kissed Abby carefully, slowly, sensually in the flickering light of the TV.

Abby felt her own lips part in response, as though her body knew what to do even as her mind was reeling. Gabrielle continued to press soft lips against her own, the faint taste of lip gloss and the Ethiopian spices making Abby dart her tongue out searching for more.

They kissed in the dark room for what seemed like hours, trading lazy kisses, deep kisses, until Abby's lips were swollen and numb. Her hands sought Gabrielle's body, knuckles brushing the soft material of her shirt, settling on her hips.

And then a heavy fist slammed on the front door.

Gabrielle jerked back, her pupils blown and lips brilliantly red. She didn't take her eyes off Abby for a moment, breathing heavily.

Then the knock on the door echoed through the apartment again, an earthquake shattering the easy intimacy between them. In a split second, the Gabrielle Abby had been kissing was no more, a statue of ice and fury taking her place.

Abby trailed after her in confusion as Gabrielle stalked to the door, tearing it open to reveal a man Abby recognized almost immediately by his scowl. The man from the gala who had glared at her from across the room after her dance with Gabrielle. Her manager.

"Where were you tonight?" he demanded, pushing his way inside the apartment.

Gabrielle didn't answer immediately. She closed the door, stepping back and putting space between them. Her posture gave nothing away, but her eyes were cold. "I told you, Darren," she said, "that I would be unavailable tonight."

"You missed an important meeting with a designer, for what?" he spat.

Abby shifted, wondering if she could slip out of the room without being noticed.

But Darren caught her movement, his enraged gaze narrowing in on her almost immediately and making Abby feel like a deer caught in headlights. Abby could imagine what he was seeing: a woman with her hair mussed, lips red, cheeks flushed.

"You canceled dinner with one of the top fashion designers in the country for a fuck?" The words were low, threatening. He did not look away from Abby.

And now Abby knew why they called her the Ice Queen, because the glare Gabrielle shot Darren was cold enough to send chills down Abby's spine. "You need to leave." Gabrielle's voice was like the most bitter winter night.

Darren finally tore his eyes away from Abby, something in Gabrielle's tone obviously making him pay attention. "This won't happen again.".

Gabrielle didn't acknowledge him.

"Don't forget, Gabrielle. I got you where you are today, and I can make everything you have vanish in the blink of an eye. You think you can keep supporting yourself and your father when no one in this city will touch you with a ten-foot pole?"

"Good night, Darren." Gabrielle bit out the words.

He opened his mouth, but then closed it as a thought visibly occurred to him. "I'll reschedule the dinner," he said, and his grin was anything but pleasant. "How about for Tuesday evening? I imagine you won't miss another meeting in the future." And then he was gone, leaving behind an unmoving statue as the door slammed.

Abby felt weak, as though she'd gone three rounds in a boxing ring. After a moment she noticed that her hands were shaking, and clenched them into fists at her side. And still Gabrielle didn't move, just stared at the closed door with all of the emotion of a Greek sculpture.

"I need to leave," Abby said.

Gabrielle didn't blink.

Abby repeated the words. "So, I'll see you later, alright?"

Finally Gabrielle turned to face Abby. At first there wasn't even recognition in the gaze, only a blankness that chilled Abby to the bone. But slowly she seemed to thaw, almost crumbling in on herself as she let her body relax.

"Abigail," she breathed. "I am so sorry that you had to witness that."

That? Abigail wasn't exactly sure what *that* was, except that it had been equal parts terrifying and disconcerting.

She had a million questions, but none of them seemed like a good idea to voice at that moment. "I think I should just go home now," she said instead.

Gabrielle took one step forward, unsteady for a moment, then another until she was standing before Abby, stopping a few inches away. She took Abby's hands in her own, running her hands over the shaking fingers. "I wish you had never seen that," she said. "He is . . ."

"Your manager," Abby finished. At Gabrielle's surprised look she nodded. "I remember, from the gala. He was angry then, too."

"He's angry too often. But I will get vengeance for this, and for much more, someday soon," Gabrielle murmured. She brought Abby's hands to her lips, kissing the back of her fingers. "I wish I could convince you to stay and finish the film, but I fear I won't be very good company. Can I call you a cab?"

Abby shook her head. "I'll be fine." She studied Gabrielle's face, taking in how her eyes were tight and lips pinched. On impulse, she leaned forward and kissed Gabrielle, rocking up on her toes to reach.

A little more tension left Gabrielle's body. "Thank you, Abigail."

c h a p t e r

Twelve

If Abby had been worried that the disastrous ending to their second date would sour things between them, she was in for a surprise. In fact, it seemed like Darren's intrusion had lit a fire under Gabrielle, switching her from cold to burning hot.

It started with texts.

Missing you this morning, came the first one, sent to Abby while she was walking into work. She responded with a *You too* and then forgot about the message as she waved hello to her co-workers.

When she got to lunch there was another text. *I also miss the feel of your lips and the softness of your skin.*

Abby blushed, remembering the way Gabrielle had kissed her the night before. It had been comforting, grounding her in the moment, a human connection that she'd been missing for too long.

I missed the chance to run my hands through your hair, Abby texted. Gabrielle's hair was long, the same dark brown as her eyes, and the ends of it had brushed against Abby's arms as they'd kissed, teasing her.

I missed the chance to feel your warmth above me, Gabrielle sent back only a moment later.

Abby was sure she was bright red all over. She waited until the end of her lunch break before responding. *I missed the chance to learn more about you.*

There wasn't another message from Gabrielle when she checked her phone again after work that evening. "So that's how it's going to be," Abby murmured, tucking the phone back away. Gabrielle was happy to talk about things, as long as those topics didn't involve her.

There was a long box with her name on it when she got home,

sitting innocently underneath the mailbox. She scooped it up along with the mail, dumped the bills on the counter with a grimace, and used her thumb to break the tape holding the lid on.

The smell hit her before the sight did. She inhaled, and sighed happily as her senses were filled with the fresh scent.

Flowers. Not roses, though; instead it was a gorgeous bouquet of large white and purple blooms that she didn't recognize.

A card sat on top, the creamy paper soft as Abby ran her fingers over it.

Sometimes I am not the best at sharing personal details.

That was it. Ten words written in careful cursive on expensive stock paper. Abby read the card a few times, then snorted.

"Understatement, babe," she said aloud.

She gathered the flowers into a vase, then tucked the card into her pocket before she made dinner. Every so often she looked over at the arrangement. A quick google search told her they were freesias, and Abby suspected they'd been chosen for the heady scent that was filling the small apartment.

Gabrielle must have sent them on very short notice, Abby realized as she pushed veggies around in a pan. Abby had texted her just after lunch, and Gabrielle had . . . felt the need to apologize, in her own way?

Jenna wasn't home yet, so Abby turned the heat down on her stir-fry and grabbed her phone. Gabrielle answered on the first ring.

"I hope you like them."

"Hello to you, too," Abby said, but she was smiling. Gabrielle was nervous? About her reaction?

"Of course. Abigail, it is so good to hear your voice. Did you receive the flowers?" Definitely nervous.

Abby laughed. "Yes, they're beautiful. Thank you."

"I want you to," Gabrielle said carefully.

"Want me to what?"

Gabrielle took an unsteady breath. "I want you to learn more about me. But it is not easy for me to share. In the past, my attempts to connect, to form a relationship with someone, did not end successfully. You have seen what happens when I bring someone new into my life."

Abby remembered Darren's furious glare fixed on her and

shuddered. The way he'd threatened Gabrielle and her father, though Abby didn't even know where to begin with that one. "Yeah. That happens often?"

"Not anymore." Gabrielle paused. "I have learned that it is best to avoid such relationships, or to hide them carefully from those who would seek to sabotage them. Darren is very . . ."

"Angry?"

A huff of laughter. "Yes, but not always. He is very good at what he does."

There was something else beneath those words, and the chill in the room intensified until Abby could feel goosebumps on her arms. "And what does he do?" she asked carefully.

"He has taken my Tuesdays away." The words were quiet, pained.

Abby leaned against the fridge, watching her food simmer. "What does that mean?" She recalled the vindictive glee on the manager's face the night before when he'd announced that he was rescheduling the meeting for Tuesday, and how Gabrielle had reacted, going utterly blank. "What happens on Tuesdays?"

"I used to act," Gabrielle said. It seemed like she was talking to herself instead of answering Abby's question, but Abby's instincts told her to stay quiet for now. "On stage, sometimes before the camera . . ."

For a moment the only sound Abby could hear was their combined breathing and the bubbling of sauce. She was about to speak, when Gabrielle spoke again.

"Tuesdays are the nights I go to a show. Any show, whatever catches my attention. Play, musical, one-man act. It is my night to remember what I have given up."

Suddenly Abby remembered their first date. Gabrielle had seemed genuinely upset when Abby had mentioned the possibility of losing her position at the library: *"I truly hope that you do not lose your dream job."* There was no doubt in Abby's mind that Gabrielle loved acting—that it was her dream job just like how working at the library was Abby's. But that realization opened up a wave of questions, and Abby had to bite her lip to keep them from spilling out.. *Why did you leave acting if you clearly love it so much? Why is your manager so angry? Is he always this controlling?*

"I apologize yet again." Gabrielle's voice changed, and Abby could imagine her pulling the shroud of ice back over, using it to find strength. "I have taken too much of your time tonight."

"It's alright," Abby said, because she wasn't sure what else to say.

But Gabrielle continued. "I should let you go. I have many things to do tonight, and I'm sure you do as well. Please accept the flowers, both as an apology for last night and as . . . a token of my affections for you."

Abby nodded, then realized Gabrielle couldn't see it. "I will, thank you.".

"I will call you later this week. Perhaps we can arrange another date. One with . . . more privacy."

Yeah, more privacy, without paparazzi sneaking photos or enraged managers bursting through the door. "That would be nice."

Gabrielle said goodbye and hung up, and Abby absently stirred her food while she tried to sort through the conversation that had just taken place.

Gabrielle's manager was a controlling asshole, that much was obvious. If he worked with Gabrielle even a fraction as much as Abby suspected, he would know what Tuesday evenings meant to her. And that malicious smirk on his face had said that he definitely knew what they meant. So he'd done it to hurt her.

Fury welled up in her chest, and she angrily dished out her food as the emotion flowed over her. This man was actively trying to hurt Gabrielle. And no matter what anyone said about her, no matter what names anyone called her, Gabrielle didn't deserve this pain. No one—even icy, cruel models—deserved to be hurt like this, but Abby was quickly learning that Gabrielle was the victim, not the Ice Queen that the world saw her as. There was warmth and tenderness buried beneath the carefully constructed persona, and Darren's actions only seemed to make Gabrielle hide her passion deeper.

Her phone rang, and she answered it without thinking. "Thought you were busy tonight," she teased.

There was pause, then a man's laughed. "Well, not the answer I was expecting."

Abby pulled the phone away from her ear and belatedly checked the caller ID. Brian, from the library. "Sorry!" she said. "Thought you were someone else."

"Clearly. Boyfriend?"

"Ah, no." She was on friendly terms with her co-workers, but not close enough to call after work for a personal chat. "What's going on?"

"Marcy's gonna announce it at the morning meeting, but I heard from a friend who works as an assistant to one of the City Councilmen." Brian's lighthearted tone had vanished. "They're laying off a bunch of people. Some of them from our branch. Trying to find a way to cut the budget back without having to close the libraries down."

Abby's stomach clenched, and she pushed her food away. "How many people?"

Brian exhaled heavily. "Not sure. They're going to cut hours too, maybe close earlier."

"But it's just starting to warm up!" Abby protested. "The evenings are when we need to be open the most!" While she rarely worked in the evenings, she knew from other librarians that they were getting busier as the after-work crowd began to brave the longer days and higher temperatures.

"I know," Brian said calmly. "I don't know who they're letting go, or what the new hours will be. My friend just warned me, and I wanted to pass it on to you so you aren't hit with it blind in the morning."

Shit. Abby took a deep breath, then another. "I thought there was still one more meeting before they were definitely deciding to close the library."

"That hasn't changed. The last meeting will be in the middle of May." Brian's voice was low, and he sighed. "Look, I just wanted to let you know. It wasn't right to keep that to myself."

"Yeah. Thank you."

"I'll see you tomorrow?"

Helplessness began to overwhelm Abby. "Yeah," she said. *But maybe not the day after that, or any day going forward.* The words were unspoken, but she could tell by the awkward silence that followed that Brian was likely thinking something similar.

Brian swallowed. "Alright. Night."

Abby set her phone down with fingers gone numb. Her chest felt tight, like she couldn't get enough oxygen in. She stumbled to a nearby chair and sank into it. *What am I going to do?* Black spots clouded her vision, clearing only when she hunched forward, tucking her head between her knees and finally managing to draw a shaky breath. *This can't be happening.* Abby sat up enough to cradle her head in her hands. Tears threatened to well up, and she rubbed her stinging eyes, shuddering. A dozen potential stories unfolded in her mind: losing her job tomorrow, or watching her colleagues lose theirs. The entire branch being shut down. Unemployment, debt, having to settle for a miserable dead-end job instead of living her dream. Having to move back in with her parents. Abby's breathing went shallow again, her heart pounding like it was trying to escape from her chest. *Is this what a panic attack feels like?*

She wasn't sure how long she sat there, but the room had grown dark by the time she was able to sit up. Her food was cold, although she wasn't really hungry anymore. She transferred it to a plastic container, left her dishes in the sink, and went to her room to lay down.

Am I going to lose my job tomorrow?

She thought about her mother, saying "*I told you so*" over brunch. Jenna, who couldn't handle the rent alone and would be in a tight place if Abby couldn't pay her half. Brian and Marcy and the other librarians.

And she thought about Gabrielle.

Gabrielle who clearly didn't have to worry about money, but had worries of her own to overcome. Gabrielle who probably didn't know who, exactly, she was dating; she probably assumed Abby was elegant like her, expensive clothing and makeup. What would she say if she knew Abby was unemployed, broke, struggling to get by? The gap between them was already a canyon; if Abby found herself out of work tomorrow it would be an ocean.

So when she had the strength to pick up her phone, it wasn't Gabrielle or her mother or Jenna who she called.

It was Nathan.

"Hey lady, what's going on? Don't you have an early bedtime?" Nathan sounded energetic, thrilled, and there was a low hum of noise behind him. Abby remembered with a guilty feeling that he had a show tonight. She'd lost track of the time while absorbed in her thoughts. A glance at the clock showed that it was going on eleven o'clock already.

"Sorry, I didn't mean to bother you," she said.

"No bother." Nathan seemed to be walking around, the rustle

of movement carrying through the phone. "Just finished the show tonight. Great performance, we had an understudy to replace Kara because she has a cold, and she really rocked it!"

Abby let Nathan's cheerful rambling wash over her. It was soothing, listening to someone else chat about unimportant topics.

"So why'd you call? It's pretty late."

"How'd you keep going, when it felt like all hope was lost?" The words slipped out before Abby could think them through.

Nathan exhaled. "Wow. That isn't where I thought this call was going to go." He didn't seem upset though, just contemplative. "You okay?"

"I'm . . . not sure?" Abby curled up on her bed, tucking her feet under the blanket. "They're laying off a bunch of library staff. We find out tomorrow who's getting cut."

"Oh, Abs." Nathan pulled the phone away from his mouth and spoke to someone, then the background noise vanished. "Sorry, I didn't want to be around the rest of the cast while we were talking about this. How'd you find out?"

Abby relayed the conversation with Brian, the panic that had welled up inside her. "I just remember in January, when we met. You were so downtrodden, but you somehow managed to keep going."

Nathan had been depressed, his entire life crumbling around him, and Abby had witnessed him pulling his life back together thread by thread until he'd managed to find happiness again. "I found a *reason* to keep going," Nathan said. "I knew that I needed to undo the mess that I'd gotten myself into. I needed to find a way to right wrongs, and to change myself for the better. So I set a goal and worked towards it."

"Getting Jason back."

"Yeah." Nathan's joy was evident, and it carried through in his voice. "And getting my own life back on track."

I need someone like that.

"A few weeks ago I thought everything was perfect in my life," Abby said. "I didn't realize things could change so much in such a short period of time."

Nathan laughed, though it wasn't a happy noise. "Yeah, I know what you mean." He paused. "Look, you know I worry about you dating Gabrielle. I don't know her myself, but what they say about her

. . . well, I worry a lot. So I have to ask."

Abby exhaled slowly. "Alright, ask."

"You've been on two dates now?" he asked. "But you don't seem thrilled about them. I get that she's not the Ice Queen that the rumor mill insists, but it doesn't sound like she's the warm spot in your life that you need right now."

Abby contemplated telling Nathan about the encounter with Gabrielle's manager, but it felt too personal, almost like a betrayal of Gabrielle's trust. "She's fine," she said. "More than fine. Nate, I know you don't believe it, but she *is* warm." She paused, then added, "But I don't get her. She's so closed off sometimes that it's like we're on two different planets. I don't mean the money and the fact that she's a celebrity and I'm just a librarian."

"Did she say that?" Nathan's tone changed, edges harsh. "That you're *just* a librarian?"

"No, not at all." In fact, Gabrielle had seemed enchanted when Abby had told her on their first date, and she clearly loved reading as much as Abby did. Plus Gabrielle had a movie collection that resembled Abby's own, and they shared a desire to travel. If Gabrielle would just open up and talk to her, Abby was convinced they would well-matched. "That part is just on me."

Nathan sighed. "Does she make you happy, Abs?" he asked.

Abby thought about the little moments: flowers and kissing and the way Gabrielle lit up the entire room when she finally let down her walls and relaxed for a few minutes. The way Gabrielle had held her the first time they'd danced, and how she'd looked at Abby like she was something truly beautiful.

"Yes."

"Then I'll support you and her until the ends of the earth," Nathan vowed. "Unless she hurts you." He didn't say *Until she hurts you*, but Abby could read beneath the words.

"I want to find a way to connect with her more," Abby said. "I want to get to know her better, and to get past the shields that she still keeps up when I'm around."

"Maybe that can be your goal. Your thing to look forward to. Bridging that space between you and Gabrielle."

There was a protest on the tip of her tongue. *I've tried to bridge the gap. Sometimes she's just too cold though.* But again that wasn't true. She'd tried a few topics, and then backed down when they hadn't worked. She'd assumed that Gabrielle was distant, closed-off, but their conversation earlier that evening had revealed more about Gabrielle than she'd expected.

"Alright." She uncurled, stretching out on her bed. "I can do that. Something to work towards, to keep my mind off of the bad things."

Nathan sounded pleased. "I'm always here for you," he said. "And so is Sara. You have a support system in place, to help catch you if you fall. But I think you need to go for it, because otherwise you're just giving up."

"Yeah." Abby sat up, wincing as she looked at the clock. "Okay."

"Abs, listen. Whatever happens tomorrow, you have your friends. And I guess you have Gabrielle, if you're going to keep pursuing a relationship with her."

Those were the words Abby needed to hear. "Thanks Nate."

chapter

Thirteen

Abby woke feeling like she'd been run over by a truck. She hit Snooze on her alarm clock, then lay beneath the covers with her eyes closed as she slowly worked towards getting out of bed.

By the time her clock buzzed again she was up and moving. A steaming hot shower went a long way to making her feel more human, and she got out of the apartment only a few minutes later than usual.

But she was dragging her feet as she headed to the bus that would take her to work. *Today's the day.* Either she'd be out a job, or some of her co-workers would be, and neither of those options appealed to her. She thought about Marcy, forced to make those decisions, and felt even worse.

But Nathan's words from the night before also hovered in the back of her mind. *Find something to work towards.* A goal. Gabrielle and a relationship. As Abby waited for a bus she pulled out her phone and sent a text.

Abby had been on two dates with Gabrielle so far, both at the other woman's invitation. But with Nathan's words coursing through her, she took the plunge and decided to meet Gabrielle halfway.

Can I take you out on a date sometime?

It was early, and Gabrielle likely wouldn't see it until later in the morning, but the act of sending it was enough to make her feel better.

She spent the rest of the bus ride thinking about the text, but arriving at work meant putting Gabrielle out of her thoughts and focusing on what was about to happen. It was immediately apparent when she walked into the library that Marcy had called in everyone to the usual morning meeting. Some of the staff who weren't scheduled to work that day were hanging out at the circulation desk, heads bowed, talking quietly. Judging by the mood in the break room, everyone knew—or at least strongly suspected—what the topic that morning was going to be.

Brian caught her as she walked in. "Today's going to be a rough one." He looked just as tired as she did, and had probably spent a restless night worrying about his own future like she had.

They usually spent the half-hour before the doors were unlocked in a quick, laid-back meeting to discuss any events for the day, before dispersing to check in books that had been dropped overnight; today they gathered in the break room in silence, Marcy standing somberly at the front.

Abby looked around at the small staff gathered. There were the six of them who were scheduled to work today: she and Brian and Marcy, the children's librarian named Ellen, and two part-time ladies who seemed confused but quickly picked up on the tension in the room. Three other employees mostly worked weekends and evenings.

"Most of you probably know that the BPL is facing some serious budget cuts coming up." Marcy didn't beat around the bush. "They've come to me with a proposed plan. And while I think it's a shit plan that'll only do more harm than good, unfortunately I'm not in a position to change it."

Brian caught her eye. Abby stared at him, numbness seeping over her.

"Effective May 23, we will be opening at noon on Monday, and two hours later on Tuesdays and Thursdays. Wednesdays we'll be closing at one o'clock. Friday through Sunday hours are currently not changing."

Ellen and Brian both sat up straight, making trying to voice their objections over the other.

"We have story time for the toddlers on Wednesday afternoons!" Ellen said. "It's wildly popular."

Brian's eyes were wide. "The GED class meets on Mondays at ten, and we're the only place around with a study room for them!"

Marcy shot them both a look that effectively silenced any additional protests. "We'll figure out a time to move it to."

There was a long, uncomfortable pause.

"The other part of this is not easy," Marcy said. She stared down at the floor as though unable to handle eye contact for the words she was about to say. "I've been told to cut staff by thirty percent."

Abby's breath caught in her throat. There was one other employee that wasn't there this morning, making their little branch ten in total. That meant three people being cut. *Three.*

"I'll be meeting with each of you one-on-one this morning to discuss this privately." Marcy folded her hands in front of her carefully, but Abby could tell they were shaking slightly. Marcy was fighting to stay calm.

That was the moment it struck home: the realization that Marcy, tough-as-nails and take-no-shit Marcy, was on the verge of tears. Before Abby had been panicking, but now she was completely numb with dread.

The meeting broke up after that, the morning staff going to start on the various opening tasks while the afternoon staff met in the break room to wait for their turn with Marcy.

Abby was distracted as she unlocked the front doors and greeted a mother and her young daughter at the door who were eagerly waiting to go explore the picture books. The smile she gave them wasn't as bright as she could typically manage; it felt like the entire library was under a dark cloud, and even the patrons over the next hour were unusually quiet, clearly picking up on the tension.

"You alright Miss Abigail?" An older gentleman handed her one of the large print mystery novels, weathered hands still steady. He was a regular, and he'd been coming to the library once a week to get a new mystery or action novel for years.

She checked the book out and managed a smile that hopefully looked genuine. "Yeah, just a rough morning.". Did she tell him and the others about the new library hours? Surely many of them already knew about the possible closure, but the change in their hours was likely going to be a serious shock . . .

Before she could make a decision, one of the afternoon staff tapped her on the shoulder. "Hey, I'm gonna take over for you here . . . your turn."

Abby said goodbye to the regular and pushed her chair back, absently relieved that her hands weren't shaking. There was no one in the breakroom, which seemed ominous; had anyone been fired yet?

Was she going to be the first?

Marcy was waiting for her, appearing ten years older, shoulders slumped. She straightened when she saw Abby though.

"Rough morning," Marcy said, unknowingly echoing Abby's own words from a moment before.

Abby just nodded, twisting her hands into knots while she waited.

"I had to let Lisa and Janet go."

The words hovered between them for a minute before they sunk in. Abby inhaled sharply. "Both of them?" The two women only worked part-time, both recent MLS graduates who had struggled to find a library job in a city with too few libraries.

Marcy's mouth was a grim line. "I put referrals in for both of them elsewhere."

"So that's two down, one to go," Abby said before she could think. Her knuckles were white from gripping her hands together too tightly.

"Yeah, one more." Marcy's mouth disappeared into the thinnest of lines. She watched Abby for what felt like an hour, but was probably only a couple of seconds. "I let Ellen go just before you came in here."

Abby's body jerked, and she rocked back in her seat. Horror blended with relief, and she wasn't sure whether to protest in outrage or let every muscle in her body go limp. She sat there trembling until she could manage to talk. "Ellen?"

"She volunteered."

And that was a curveball Abby hadn't expected.

Marcy kept talking. "She has two kids at home and her husband makes enough to support the whole family."

Blood rushed through Abby's ears. *Safe*, it said. *For today, you are safe*. "So I'm not fired."

Marcy cocked a shoulder. "Not unless you want to be."

"No," Abby squeaked. She cleared her throat, then tried again. "No. That's okay."

"Then get back out there. I'll have you help Ellen with the children's section today, so you can start learning what she does over there. Introduce yourself to some of the parents during story time, make sure they know you."

"Alright." Abby stood, legs shaking only a little. "Thanks Marce."

Marcy opened her mouth, then closed it. "Send Brian in," she said, and returned to staring at her desk as though the weight of the world was on her shoulders.

Abby checked her phone before going back out to find Brian and Ellen. There was a response from Gabrielle waiting.

Yes, absolutely. Just tell me when and where.

Abby gripped the phone. She pulled her shoulders back and drew strength from that message.

She was going to keep her job. She was going to prove that she could take over for Ellen, that she was worth keeping. And she was going to prove herself to Gabrielle too.

She was going to take Gabrielle Levesque on a date.

The rest of the day was exhausting. Abby hadn't slept more than a few hours the night before, and by lunchtime she was tempted to curl up under the circulation desk in search of some much-needed rest. She downed a soda and ran across the street to a coffee shop that served lunch sandwiches, then spent the rest of her lunch break texting Nathan and Gabrielle.

Nathan was obviously worried about her after their call the night before. He kept sending her funny memes and links to uplifting articles, while she tried to reassure him that she was fine.

NATHAN: *yeah sorry not buyin it. after last night the only way you'd be fine is if you had your memory erased.*

ABBY: *really, memory jokes from you?*

NATHAN: *yep, but i'm the only one allowed to make them, don't forget it.*

ABBY: *you're terrible*

NATHAN: *terribly hilarious*

Abby rolled her eyes at the phone. Nathan's amnesia was something they could smile about now, but she'd met him right as he was recovering—both from the accident and from the aftermath of telling Jason what he'd remembered.

ABBY: *I am okay though. promise. And I texted gabrielle this morning to ask her out on a date on my terms.*

NATHAN: *good. do something that you're comfortable with.*

maybe a more relaxing date will help her open up with you!

But that was the problem. Now that Gabrielle had accepted her invitation, she had to come up with an actual place for them to go.

So she texted Gabrielle: *Is there a play you want to see that you haven't yet?*

Gabrielle's responded almost immediately with a list of plays and musicals that Abby recognized. A quick search online told her that most of them were sold out, and she couldn't afford tickets to any of the ones that weren't.

Well, that idea was out.

Then she had to set her phone aside and get back to work.

Still, the day was starting to look up. She hadn't been fired, and she had a date.

Then Marcy passed her an envelope, which she made the mistake of opening at her desk, and the day went from okay to far worse.

"This is a joke, right?" she asked a minute later, leaning her shoulder against the door of Marcy's office.

Marcy looked even more drawn, bags beneath her eyes. "I wish it was."

"I pretty much live paycheck to paycheck as it is," Abby pointed out. She took a deep breath; this wasn't Marcy's fault, and her boss was just as upset as she was, but still. "Cutting my hours back *and* cutting wages?"

"The budget they've given us to work with is only one step above no budget at all," Marcy said. "You're not the only one getting a pay cut."

Brian took that moment to storm in. "Marce, this was sitting on my desk when I got back from lunch."

He was holding an envelope identical to Abby's.

After a lengthy conversation that left all three of them in worse moods than before, Abby went to help Ellen with the children's section. She'd never assisted with story time, and was nervous about taking over for Ellen.

She hadn't been expecting parents who were upset and baffled by the newly-announced schedule changes, which Marcy had posted on the library doors over lunch.

And she definitely hadn't expected the children.

When Ellen gently announced that Wednesday Story Time would be moving to another day, two kids started crying. Abby gave Ellen a horrified look as a third kid joined in, and the room suddenly got very loud.

But Ellen was clearly adept at handling temper tantrums and upset children. She took charge, soothing the crying and launching into a story that soon had the kids captivated and smiling again.

After, she pulled Abby aside. "A lot of these kids get dropped off by parents desperate for an hour of free babysitting," she said. "This is their time to see other kids their age and hear a story, and for a five or six year old that's pretty huge."

"I'm don't know how to handle kids the way you do," Abby confessed.

"You'll learn," Ellen assured her.

But the event left a sour taste in Abby's mouth. She wasn't sure that she could calm a group of emotional children, or deftly reroute an angry parent like Ellen had done.

By mid-afternoon Abby was inundated with patrons asking her questions about the announcements taped to the doors. She stayed late that evening, helping the closing shift with tasks that had been overlooked or ignored during the day.

It wasn't until she was on her way home that she had a chance to check her phone again. There was a text from Gabrielle.

I don't care what we do on our date, as long as I can spend it learning more about you.

Abby re-read the message and smiled. Gabrielle could be very sweet at times, and moments like these were enough to provide a small ray of light in an otherwise dark day.

But the text also fueled her desire to make the date a perfect one. She wanted to make Gabrielle smile as well, and wanted to get to know Gabrielle as much as the other woman wanted to get to know her.

She just had to make it through the rest of the week at work, and then she could see Gabrielle and hopefully have a relaxing weekend. By the time she collapsed into bed that night, Abby had a plan for the next few days: survive, try not to cry (or make any kids cry), and figure out somewhere special to take Gabrielle on their date.

chapter

Fourteen

S he was a librarian in Brooklyn, scraping by. It was insanity, to
think she could take Gabrielle on a date that wouldn't be terrible,
or showcase exactly how broke she was. Of course she couldn't take
her to another fancy restaurant, or to an apartment like Gabrielle's
expansive (and expensive) loft. The former was well outside her price-
range, and the latter . . . she tried to imagine Gabrielle in her tiny
apartment, but the mental image simply didn't compute.

"Where'd you take your girlfriend on your first date?" she asked
Brian.

"Concert at the Barclay Center. We had a few too many beers, left
during the encore to head back to my place. Why?"

Abby sighed and texted Nathan.

Where do you and Jason go on dates?

Nathan responded a few hours later. *Kinda depends. If it's up to
him we go to a Yankees game, or there's this steak restaurant that we
always go to if he wants to be really romantic.*

Another dead end.

Sara was slightly more helpful, although she was also the only one
to catch on to why Abby was calling. "What does she like?" Sara asked.

Abby started to shrug, then hesitated. "Ethnic food," she said.
"Geeky movies. Theater." *And books.* That was important, but Abby
didn't know how to build a date around a mutual love of reading.

Sara '*hmmmm*ed' over the phone. "So find something to do with
one of those."

"Easier said than done," Abby shot back.

"Nothing worth doing is easy."

"Did you seriously just misquote Theodore Roosevelt at me?"

Abby protested.

Sara scoffed. "Please," she said. "I got that from Pinterest. Now stop being desperate and put that big brain of yours to work."

Abby let Sara hang up on her without further objection, and got to work. She flipped through the paper at her desk, looking for upcoming events. She searched online, and asked around with her colleagues.

It was Jenna who came up with the answer. "You want cheap and delicious," she said.

"Well, duh."

Jenna hushed her. "Smorgasburg."

"Gesundheit."

"It's the local food festival. It's running every weekend now that it's warmed up a bit. Eclectic, lots of choice, and generally just a really fun time."

Abby considered it for a second. "I think I read about it." She pulled it up on her phone, browsing through the pictures of weird and delicious offerings. It seemed like it might be crowded, but perfect for people watching, and the idea of wandering around and trying new foods with Gabrielle was incredibly appealing. "Alright, you win."

Jenna grinned. "You ever gonna tell me about this date of yours?"

"Maybe soon." Abby was, in fact, dreading the conversation in which she told her roommate (and, eventually, her parents) about the renowned supermodel that she was possibly-sort-of dating. "Let's see how this date goes first."

She texted Gabrielle before she could think twice. *Want to come out to my neck of the woods next Sunday for a street food festival?*

Gabrielle responded almost immediately. *I wouldn't miss it for the world.*

The Saturday before their date brought clear blue skies and a warm sun that made it feel as if Spring had truly arrived. The weather looked to hold all weekend, and Abby couldn't help but text Gabrielle that morning.

They have a ramen burger.

Gabrielle responded with a selfie of her face scrunched up as though she'd smelled something bad , which made Abby laugh.

Okay, we'll skip the ramen burger then. They also have coffee with mushrooms?

I'll give any coffee at least one try, Gabrielle sent a few seconds later.

They went back and forth all morning, Abby looking up the vendors and getting more and more excited, and Gabrielle seeming to share her enthusiasm.

What's the strangest food you've ever tried? Abby asked.

Gabrielle apparently didn't need to think hard about that. *Fugu.*

Abby had to google it before responding. *You ate poisonous fish? Why?!*

It is a specialty, and not poisonous when prepared correctly. But not one I would like to risk trying again.

And then, early in the afternoon, the texts dried up.

Abby waited an hour before sending her another message. She sent another at dinner, just making sure everything was alright. Gabrielle hadn't been busy that day, and hadn't mentioned any evening plans.

She tried calling before bed, but the phone rang to voicemail. Abby ended the call instead of leaving a message; either something had come up, or Gabrielle had decided Abby was being annoying and was ignoring her. Her mind refused to accept any other alternatives.

She fell asleep without receiving any further messages.

When her alarm went off the next morning, though, there was a text waiting for her.

I am afraid I must cancel our outing today, Abigail. My sincerest apologies.

Abby stared at the phone. The text had come around midnight.

Oh. Okay. She hit Send on the reply, then tossed the phone on her bed and tucked her knees under her chin.

"How the hell did I mess that up so quickly?" Had she sent too many texts? But Gabrielle had been responding, up until the moment she wasn't. "Maybe she was hoping for something higher-class. Or less crowded. Or just different."

The morning was looking to be another beautiful one, but Abby only wanted to curl back up in bed and catch a few extra hours of sleep.

Her phone rang.

Gabrielle.

"I am sorry." Gabrielle sounded out of breath, tired, her accent stronger than usual. "Oh Abigail, please forgive me. I can't . . ." she took inhaled deeply over the line.

"It's okay," Abby said, the words flat even to her own ears.

"It's not," Gabrielle said. "I have been scheduled to replace someone at a photoshoot today. The other model, she is very sick, so my manager has arranged for me to take her place." A pause. "They have already been told to expect me. I cannot get out of it."

There was something in her tone at the end there that caught Abby's attention. "He did this on purpose."

A long silence. Then, "Yes."

"Why?"

Gabrielle didn't speak.

"Okay." Abby sat up straighter in bed. "Alright. We can reschedule. Try again next weekend."

"No." Gabrielle said the single word viciously. "I will not let him win this one."

"It's not a war."

"Oh, Abigail, but it is. He has pulled ahead with this battle, but I will not be defeated." Gabrielle sounded stronger, more resolute with every word. "Come with me to the photoshoot. I must be there at ten o'clock for makeup and wardrobe. Come spend the day with me. I don't promise it will be as fun as your food festival, but I would see you again and show Darren that he has not won today."

Abby thought about the night at Gabrielle's apartment, and the way Darren had glared at her. Maybe it wasn't a war, but Darren definitely believed he was winning something. And the idea of seeing Gabrielle sounded good, even if it wasn't the date Abby had expected. She checked her clock: Just past eight.

"Yeah, okay. Where and when?"

There were still clothes from Sara's closet in her own, left there during their last wardrobe consultation. Abby flipped through them, finding a sundress that looked cute with a pair of her own flats. She researched a few makeup tutorials on YouTube and practiced until she began to resemble the fictional creature she'd first become the night of the gala.

The jeans and worn button-down she'd been planning to wear to the food festival were thrown over a chair, at odds with the mask she was slowly putting on now. But she was stepping back into Gabrielle's world, and that meant the real Abby would have to hide for another day.

She left with enough time to take the train to the location Gabrielle had given her, walking the last few blocks to a park. Security was set up around the area, as were several trucks with such ominous names as Makeup, Catering, and Director.

Abby had been picturing a few men with cameras. This seemed like an entire movie production.

She texted Gabrielle rather than braving the glaring security guards, and felt palpable relief when she spotted the long dark hair towering over the rest of the crowd.

"Abigail." Gabrielle held an arm out, pulling Abby in close. She pressed a kiss to the skin beneath her ear, then breathed, "Thank you for coming today."

Gabrielle was already made-up, and she appeared ethereal in the sunlight, copper shine glittering on her skin from powder. She twined their fingers together right there in public, and led Abby into the set, moving easily around camera gear and large screens that might have had something to do with changing the lighting.

The entire park had been taken over by the photoshoot. A crew was hanging lanterns and gauzy fabric from the trees, and . . . "Is that man painting the leaves?"

"It's a temporary water-based paint," Gabrielle said. When Abby glanced over, she noticed the Gabrielle was staring straight ahead as they walked, hyper-focused on the path in front of her.

"But why?" She could see scatterings of color in all of the trees now that she looked, browns and oranges. "It's like they're pretending it's autumn."

Gabrielle still didn't turn to see what Abby was talking about, and Abby realized her shoulders were squared, sharp lines prepared to cut anyone who approached her. This was the Ice Queen returning, someone Abby had only seen in fragments in the past.

But Gabrielle didn't let go of her hand. Abby squeezed it gently, and felt an answering pulse a moment later.

"This shoot is for an autumn catalogue," Gabrielle explained. "It is much worse in winter, when we must film for the summer spreads. They will correct the photos digitally, and turn this lovely spring morning into a perfect fall day."

Abby had a dozen more questions, but Gabrielle was slowing in front of one of the trailers, where a black canvas chair was propped next to a table that made Laura's makeup collection look like a five-year-old playing pretend.

"You're already wearing makeup," Abby pointed out.

Gabrielle gave her hand one last squeeze, then let go. "The process has only just begun."

Sure enough, two women descended on Gabrielle the moment they spotted her, and a man bearing an impressive array of hair brushes and straighteners followed a moment later. Abby found a place out of the way to perch, watching as other models began to trickle in. There were four in total, and they alternated between being teased and tweezed to perfection and relaxing with their phones and earbuds when the stylists moved on to another model for a while.

All of them relaxed, that was, except Gabrielle. She sat straight, somehow managing to appear rigid and imposing while also having an irreverent attitude that plainly said she had better places to be right now. She didn't look over at Abby, and she didn't speak, but Abby knew she was aware of everything going on around her.

"Hey." One of the models snapped, and Abby turned to her in surprise. She was a waif of a girl, all wrist bones and pale, pale skin. "Get me a Venti Skinny Mocha."

"Excuse me?" Abby blinked.

"I mean, you're just standing there. Make yourself useful."

"I'm not . . ."

But Gabrielle was there suddenly, towering over the tiny girl with fury etched in every line of her body. "You don't speak to her.".

"What the hell do you—"

"Quiet." Gabrielle wasn't shouting, but her voice was icy enough to carry, and everyone paused to watch. "You don't speak to her. She is here with me. And given the rumor that they had to go up a size for your clothing for this shoot, I would lay off the dairy products, hm?"

There was a gasp from one of the other models, equally shocked and delighted, and the tiny woman who had snapped at Abby went scarlet.

Gabrielle stared down at her coolly, driving home the point in silence. Then she glanced at Abby, nodded once, and returned to her seat. She looked like a goddess, carved from dark stone. Abby couldn't pull her eyes away.

The stylists slowly returned to work, but this time Abby had the unsettling awareness that everyone was watching her out of the corner of their eyes. Trying to figure out who she was, why she was there. Judging her.

Abby had thought she was out of place that night at Printemps. She'd been wrong; *this* was what it felt like to not belong.

The hair and makeup team finished their work, and then the models were brought to wardrobe. They were fitted, accessorized, touched-up with more hair and makeup. Abby trailed behind them, and no one said anything to her when she found a few empty lighting cases to lean against.

It should have been boring to watch four women have their pictures taken for hours, but instead it was fascinating. People scurried around in a well-rehearsed dance, and a single colored filter over a light could change the entire mood of the set. Abby didn't care about the clothes and the setting, but the way the photographers worked to capture each shot was intriguing, and she kept watching a man who must be the shoot director as he yelled instructions.

"But what could she be getting from it?"

Abby didn't turn at the words, assuming she'd caught part of a conversation that she wasn't involved in. A glance showed that two of the models from the stylists' trailer earlier had stopped just a few feet away from her.

"No idea," the other girl answered. "I mean, she's pretty enough I guess, but really kind of plain?"

And now Abby had a feeling they were talking about her and Gabrielle after all.

The first woman laughed harshly. "That's what she does after all, right?" she asked. "Fucks 'em to get something from them, and then leaves them behind?"

When she peeked out of the corner of her eye again, both of the women were staring right at her. Abby swallowed. She was suddenly aware that they were doing this on purpose, making sure she could hear the entire conversation.

"I feel sorry for her," the second woman said. "I mean, she probably has no idea what she's gotten herself into, just like all the others. Hopefully she'll get out before Gabrielle uses her and tosses her aside her like the rest of them."

They walked off then, and Abby stood perfectly still, trying to figure out what, exactly, she'd heard. A warning? *Are they saying that Gabrielle is only using me for sex?* But they weren't having sex, and she couldn't see what else Gabrielle might be using her for.

She pushed the conversation aside, determined not to let strangers ruin the few salvageable parts of the day. Like people-watching, and learning more about an industry that she'd known nothing about. And she went back to watching Gabrielle, too, though the pleasure of seeing her was tempered by the chill Abby got every time their eyes met.

Because *this* was the Gabrielle that everyone else knew. The one Abby had only heard rumors of, warnings.

Gabrielle was fierce in her own way. She stood out among the other women in the shoot, her skin and hair darker than the blonde, blue-eyed women around her. It was clearly purposeful, a contrast of coloring, and Abby knew all eyes would be drawn to her when the photos appeared in magazines and on websites. If she hadn't already been watching her so intently, it would be impossible to look anywhere else.

She was so absorbed in her study of Gabrielle the Ice Queen that she didn't notice someone standing next to her until they spoke.

"I'm not sure what the hell you're doing here."

Abby didn't need to look over to recognize that voice. Gabrielle's manager was taller than her, a dark figure looming over Abby out of the corner of her eye.

"I'm here at Gabrielle's invitation," Abby said. "It seems like *someone* scheduled her for this shoot when she already had plans, and I wasn't going to turn down the chance to see her again."

"I'd have you removed from this set in a heartbeat if I didn't think she'd cause a scene." Darren spoke calmly, like they were having a polite conversation, and it was somehow even worse than when he'd been vicious and cruel. Abby had to use every ounce of her willpower to not turn her head, focusing on Gabrielle like a lifeline. Across the room, Gabrielle's face changed minutely when she glanced in their direction, a flash of anger that the photographer immediately pounced on. Darren's next words ripped through Abby's focus. "Whores like you don't belong here."

"Excuse me?" Abby couldn't stop herself from turning now.

Darren smirked and folded his arms. "You heard me. I don't care what you're getting out of sleeping with her. Fame? Maybe you like the attention. Whatever it is, you don't belong here."

"I think that's for Gabrielle to decide," Abby said, but the words were a thin mask for the twisting in her stomach. Darren was only saying things that she'd already thought multiple times that day.

"Gabrielle might enjoy fucking the peasants every so often," Darren said. "But you'll only keep her attention for a short time. She's going to be the next big name; this shoot is nothing, just a stepping stone. You think she got to where she is today by having an ugly little thing like you at her side?"

"Shut up," Abby said, biting back tears.

But Darren had obviously latched on to the perceived weakness, a shark circling for the kill. "Gabrielle knows where her best interests lie: with me. She also knows where she should lie: also with me. You're her temper tantrum." He must have spotted the disbelief on Abby's face. "Oh yes, that's all you are. She's upset with me, so you're a distraction. She'll be back in my bed soon enough, once she's done with you."

"I think you're wrong." But Abby's voice wavered on the words as she swallowed back tears.

"You can think whatever you want." Darren finally looked away, and it was like a physical weight lifted from Abby. He was watching Gabrielle now, and Abby followed his gaze. Gabrielle who was in the middle of the shoot and unable to get away, but her eyes flickered to the two of them every time there was a pause in the photographing.

"Enjoy your day on the set, little slut. Your fifteen minutes of fucking a celebrity are coming to an end."

"We're not having sex," Abby said, but Darren had already walked off, pulling his phone out and tapping away without turning back. Abby found an empty chair and collapsed into it. She could ignore the two models, but ignoring Darren was like ignoring a raging bull standing before her.

Is that what they think of me? That I'm just here because I'm sleeping with Gabrielle? That Gabrielle is just using me for sex? But it didn't make any sense, because so far Gabrielle hadn't pushed her into having sex.

Does Gabrielle really use people like everyone says? She doesn't seem like that type of person. Another thought, right on the tail end of that one: *But then, do I actually know her at all?*

chapter

Fifteen

The photoshoot was anticlimactic after that; Darren avoided both Abby and Gabrielle, lingering at the edge of the shoot untilthe makeup and clothes had been removed and the cameras put away. It was late afternoon when Abby joined Gabrielle outside of the costume trailer; the other woman looked frayed around the edges, skin red from the makeup remover and eyes soft with exhaustion.

"What did he say to you?" Gabrielle asked.

The question stung. After they'd barely spoken all day while Abby had sat on the sidelines and watched Gabrielle work, this was the first thing Gabrielle asked? "Nothing important," Abby said.

If Gabrielle picked up on the lie, she was too tired to try and dig beneath it. "Thank you for coming today."

Better, though it was clearly still the Ice Queen speaking to her and not Gabrielle. "It was interesting to observe the shoot," she said honestly.

"It gets boring when you do it often. A long day of standing around doing nothing, interspersed with moments of rushing. Tiring."

"It was a look into a new world" *A world I definitely do not fit into.* "I never knew this much work went into a couple of pictures in a magazine."

Gabrielle gave her a tight smile. "I am glad you were here. I should get home and rest now."

It was a dismissal, as plain as anything. And it hurt more than Gabrielle's flat responses.

"Alright. I'll see you later." Abby hesitated, lingering awkwardly. Did she give Gabrielle a hug? A kiss? But Gabrielle just turned and vanished behind a trailer, and Abby was left alone.

Going home seemed like an impossible option; how could she sit around on the couch and enjoy the rest of the afternoon with Darren's words rattling around in her head and Gabrielle's vacant responses stinging her skin?

The only thing Abby could think to do was find a distraction, and there was one easy method of doing so. She sent her a text to her mother, letting her know she was going to stop by for dinner, and made her way to the nearest LIRR station.

The train was almost empty heading out to Long Island at that time of the afternoon, and Abby leaned her head against the window to watch the familiar towns roll past. She tried to focus on other things, but her mind kept circling back to Gabrielle. Dancing with her at the gala had been like fanning a spark, though the meal at the restaurant had cooled it to a smoldering ember. But the second date at Gabrielle's apartment had been explosive by the end. Before Darren had interrupted.

Yeah, but what happens when she realizes that I won't *sleep with her?* It was a bucket of cold water on Abby's thoughts, and she sat up in her seat. Of course that would be the end of the relationship. Even though Gabrielle hadn't pushed her, it seemed clear that she wanted to have sex. Abby didn't—couldn't—know her very well, but what she'd gleaned from other people and her own observations told her that Gabrielle had a lot of sex. And everyone else sure seemed to think they were sleeping together—especially Darren.

And what the hell is his problem? She's been called a lot of things by a lot of people: a prude or bitch from dates who'd wanted to take the relationship beyond platonic. 'Strange' by her mother, wondering why her daughter didn't ever go out with anyone. But never a slut or a whore.

It seemed like everyone had things backwards. She and Gabrielle weren't having sex, but everyone assumed they were. Gabrielle wasn't the cruel one, but Darren was.

By the time the train pulled into the station, Abby had figured out a few things:

First, it was pretty obvious that she and Gabrielle were not meant to be. The interests they had in common were fantastic, and there was no denying that Abby felt a spark whenever she was around Gabrielle, but they existed in two different universes and there was no bridge on earth big enough to connect them. If Abby didn't break if off soon, she'd have her heart broken when Gabrielle realized the relationship was never going to make it to the bedroom.

Second, if Darren was to be believed, he and Gabrielle had dated at one point. Or just slept together? Abby was still confused by the whole sex-but-no-emotions concept. But she had a feeling that his vicious comments came from jealousy, and a romantic relationship seemed like the only reasonable explanation.

Her mother was waiting on the street below the platform when the train pulled in, and Abby slid into the car silently and let her mom chat about her women's group and the antique market while they drove home. "We were going to have leftovers for dinner tonight," she said as they pulled into the driveway, "but your dad decided to make a roast when he heard you were coming over. It'll be another hour probably."

"Good." They pulled into the driveway, and Abby jumped out of the car and stared up at the house she'd grown up in. Her mother unlocked the door, holding it open so Abby could walk in and kick off her shoes.

"So what brings you out here this evening?"

Abby considered her options. She could tell her mother a sanitized version of her not-relationship with Gabrielle, or let her mother rant about the library for the rest of the evening. The former seemed like the better choice if she didn't want another round of *All those student loans have been for nothing*.

"I've kind of been seeing someone?" she began tentatively.

Her mother crossed herself dramatically. "Oh, thank the heavens." She raised her voice to carry through the house. "Jacob, I'm taking Abby out to the back yard with a bottle of wine for some mother-daughter bonding time."

"Mom," Abby said, eyes wide.

"Abigail, I have waited almost three decades for you to come to me to talk about dating . . . or, dare I hope, bring someone home for us to meet. Let me savor this moment."

Abby didn't move.

"Abigail, get your ass into the backyard and start talking, because

I swear every mothering gene in my body just activated and I need details of the relationship that finally brought you to my door for advice." Her mother had her hands on her hips, and a look on her face that told Abby she'd made a terrible miscalculation; the library suddenly seemed a much safer topic.

But it was too late now, so Abby let her mother ply her with wine, a spinach dip she'd found in the fridge, and she gave up the story about meeting Gabrielle at the gala and how they'd gone on out for dinner to a fancy restaurant in Manhattan.

Her mother had never had a problem with Abby's biromanticism, and she swooned dramatically when Abby mentioned Gabrielle's name. "My daughter, dating a super model!" she proclaimed. She was clearly channeling her inner Scarlett O'Hara tonight . . . or she'd had too much wine already. "The ladies in my book club are going to be so jealous!"

"So . . . that's the thing, mom," Abby said. "I'm not actually sure that we are dating. Or that I want to be dating her."

Her mother waited with uncharacteristic patience.

"I mean, she's sort of a celebrity," Abby said. "I went to a fashion shoot with her today, and I've never felt so out of place. I think I was hoping it would be like a romance novel, where the poor librarian is swept off her feet by the rich model, but I can't get over how different our lives are."

"But do you like her?" Her mother propped her elbows up on the table. "Specifically, do you like her as a person, not as a model?"

Abby thought before answering. There was definitely a lot about Gabrielle the Person to like, and moments between them that made her smile to recall. The memory of Gabrielle's warm ankle against her own, the way she never pushed Abby for anything beyond what Abby was willing to give. The collection of geeky movies hidden under her TV, and the confession that she loved to read science fiction and fantasy novels. The way her eyes, so cold when facing the rest of the world, softened when she looked at Abby.

"Yes," Abby said honestly. "But I don't know if that's enough." *How important is sex? Because it seems like everyone keeps bringing it up, and I'm pretty sure it's going to be a deal-breaker.*

Her dad stuck his head out, calling them in for dinner. Her

mother dusted off her hands and grabbed the half-empty bottle of wine. "I know you don't listen to my advice," she said, pushing back the deck chair and standing. "God only knows you'd be in a much more stable job if you did."

"Mom."

"But you have never in your entire life come to talk to me about a woman *or* a man, Abigail. So this Gabrielle, she must mean something to you. And if you want my advice, I say find a way to keep her. Find the compromise, or risk losing someone you've clearly connected with."

Abby stayed sitting for another minute, deep in thought while her mother walked back into the house.

chapter

Sixteen

She didn't talk to Gabrielle for three days after that. When she got home from her parents' that night there was a single text from Gabrielle wishing her a good night, but Abby turned her phone to silent and set it aside, pretending she hadn't seen it.

It was the coward's way out, and she knew it, but there were too many thoughts racing through her mind at the moment and she needed to figure herself out before figuring out her relationship.

Apparently figuring herself out required a lot of greasy fries, because two days after the photo shoot she found herself sitting on a fake leather bench at the diner where Sara worked.

"I have no idea why anyone comes to me with relationship advice," Sara said, setting down a basket of fries and two sodas before sliding into the booth, across from her. "It's not like I've had the best run of luck with the men I've dated."

"Maybe you should give the ladies a try then," Abby teased.

Sara laughed, rolling her eyes. "You're hilarious. So, what's up?"

Whereas Abby had held back on telling her mother the details about her and Gabrielle's roller coaster relationship, she filled Sara in without hesitation.

Sara let out a low whistle. "What a dick," she said, when Abby finished telling her about Gabrielle's manager. "Sounds like you should just run while you can. She may not be the Ice Queen that Nate was warning you about, but she's clearly got some issues, and the way she treated you at the photo shoot was pretty awful."

"That's what I have to decide."

"Okay, the cons are obvious enough," Sara said, kicking her feet up on the bench and leaning back against the wall. "What are the pros?"

Abby swiped a French fry through ketchup and bit down on it, chewing while thinking. "We actually have a lot in common. We like the same movies, read the same books. There's definitely an emotional link there. And," She blushed, taking a sip of her soda to try and hide it, "we made out on her couch once and it was really awesome."

Sara's legs swung off the seat and hit the ground with a loud thump. "There was making out?" she asked, too loudly. "And you didn't tell me?"

Abby glanced around, hoping no one was paying attention to them. The diner was thankfully mostly empty, though a table of older women gave them amused looks. "Keep your voice down," she said. "Yeah, there was making out. Once. Briefly. We got interrupted."

"I thought you didn't do that. Like, kissing and stuff."

Abby took another fry. "Kissing is nice," she said. "And Gabrielle is a really good kisser. It's not foreplay for me or anything." She was bright red right now, and she knew it, "But I like the connection."

Sara nodded. "Okay, so the kissing is a definite Pro. What else?"

"I think she's fascinating," Abby admitted. "I mean, I've never met anyone like her. Normally I can come up with people's stories by looking at them. Even if it's not their real story, it's enough to satisfy me, so I don't need to keep guessing. But she . . . keeps me guessing."

"And she's super hot," Sara said, using a fry to emphasize her point.

"And she's super hot," Abby conceded with a grin.

"And she likes you."

Abby shrugged. "I think she does."

"I'm not exactly the poster child for stable relationships," Sara said. "But it sounds like you should give her another chance. One more chance, to tip the scales one way or another."

"My mom said something similar," Abby admitted.

Sara snagged the last of the fries with a flourish. "So give her another try. Send her a text tomorrow and see if she'll reschedule your date."

Yeah, I can do that. Abby took a sip from her drink.. *One more try. A date without Darren, without interruptions.*

Abby intended to call Gabrielle the next day. She woke up that morning, got ready for work, and started typing a text on her way to the library. Half a dozen unsent drafts later, she conceded that a text was probably not the best way to say, *Hey, sorry for ignoring you for two days, but I've been really conflicted since the weekend and want to go on one more date before I decide if I want to keep dating you.*

A call when she took a break mid-morning would be a better option, maybe.

Except that everything went wrong from the moment she got into the library.

The computer system had gone offline the evening before, and there was a massive stack of books and media to check back in once the system came back up that morning. A small child threw up in the middle of the circulation area before the library had been open for more than an hour, leaving a terrible acidic smell lingering all morning.

And Marcy and Brian were in foul moods, glowering and silent.

"Okay, what the hell is going on?" Abby asked, cornering Brian when she went on lunch. She felt frazzled, trying to do her usual tasks as well as helping out in the children's section, and the black cloud hanging over the library that morning wasn't helping.

Brian glanced up from the stack of mail he was sorting through. "The fact that you don't keep up with the news amazes me."

"Because you normally just tell me if there's anything I should know. Plus, I can at least figure out if it's good or bad by the level of emo you're radiating." Abby folded her arms. "Now tell me, or go into the office to finish what you're doing. You're going to start scaring the patrons away."

"Pretty sure the smell is doing that for us."

Abby put her hands on her hips. "Stop avoiding the question," she said. "I'm an only child with an over-bearing mother. I'm a master at avoidance."

Brian sighed and set down his work. "The city council meeting was last night," he said.

"Oh." There was a four-letter word that Abby desperately wanted to add to the end of that, but she managed to swallow it at the last second. "It didn't go well then."

"No. They're going ahead with the closures. Marcy's so upset that she won't even talk about it. She told me to make sure everyone knew, but . . ." His face made it clear that he was struggling to bring the topic up as well.

"Fuck." Abby breathed the word, unable to hide her dismay any longer.

Brian looked grim. "The June council meeting is June 14. They'll be ratifying the budget then, so we'll have a week after that to close down once it's confirmed."

Any thought of calling Gabrielle fled from Abby's mind, and she found herself in the same bad mood as her co-workers. Marcy pulled her from the check-out desk after lunch to start revising the schedule for June on the library website, then disappeared back into her office to make a series of phone calls that only seemed to sour her mood further.

By three o'clock, Abby was ready to escape the library. She'd never been one of those people who was eager to leave work as soon as the clocked ticked past quitting time, but today four thirty couldn't come soon enough.

She was hunched over a trade journal at the circulation desk, flipping idly through the pages, when someone in front of her cleared their throat.

"You've been ignoring me for three days, Abigail."

Abby's head shot up, eyes wide. *I'm dreaming*, she thought with alarm. *I fell asleep at the desk, that's all.*

"Either you're trying to break up with me, or you're upset with me, but I must know which is the case so I can try to beg for your forgiveness." Nope, not dreaming. Gabrielle Levesque was standing in the middle of the Brooklyn Public Library, as radiant as ever.

"Gabrielle," she said.

Gabrielle tilted her head. "So you have not forgotten who I am. That was my other theory. I've read many novels where the love interest loses their memories, after all."

"Love interest?" Abby squeaked, her mind still struggling to process Gabrielle's sudden appearance at her workplace.

Gabrielle smiled faintly. "Let's come back to that one."

Abby's mind finally caught up with her and she stood up quickly. "I didn't expect to see you," she said. "I'm just . . . what are you doing here?"

"I texted and called, but you didn't answer," Gabrielle said. "I did not think flowers would be an adequate apology this time, so I needed to see you in person."

"Okay." Abby stared up at her, still struggling to make sense of the situation.

Gabrielle propped her hip against the desk, closing the distance between them. "I still had your address," she said. "And I knew you worked for the library, so I began phoning each branch until I found the one you worked at."

That answered the *how* and the *why* at least.

And now Gabrielle was giving her a genuine smile. "I admit, I enjoy surprising you like this. I hope it's a good surprise, but . . . it is *very* good to see you, Abigail."

Oh shit. Abby was mortified; she was in her work clothes— black slacks and a dark red button-down that probably had a few wrinkles in it from being hung up badly. She wasn't wearing any makeup, and her hair was all over from having run her hands through it in frustration that day.

And Gabrielle was standing in front of her, wearing a form-fitting pantsuit and heels, not a strand of hair out of place, as if she was fresh off the runway.

Gabrielle's smile began to fade, and Abby realized that she was waiting for a response.

"It's . . . it's good to see you too," she said. "Really, it is. It's just been a stressful day. I meant to call you this morning actually, but things have been insane and I didn't have time. I'm so sorry you had to come all the way out here. I didn't mean to ignore you, I promise."

She said all of this very quickly.

Gabrielle put a hand over her own and met her gaze, bringing Abby's attention to the fact that she had clenched her hands into fists.

Abby took a deep breath. "If I'd known you were coming, I would have cleaned myself up a bit." She probably had an old eyeliner pen and some lip gloss in her bag.

"You look perfect." Gabrielle didn't break eye contact.

Abby blushed.

"Do you work much later?" Gabrielle asked. "I suspect we need to talk."

"Just another hour or so," Abby said softly.

Gabrielle nodded as though she'd expected this. "I am going to find somewhere to sit and read until you are done," she said. "I will come back here in an hour."

She squeezed Abby's hand beneath her own, brushed a there-and-gone kiss over the corner of her mouth, then turned and vanished into the stacks.

Abby stood there for another moment, trying to figure out what had just happened.

"That was Gabrielle Levesque." Brian's awed voice snapped Abby out of her thoughts.

She looked over to see him standing beside her, his gaze following the path Gabrielle had just taken. "What?"

Brian was watching her at her intently. "Gabrielle Levesque. She's on a billboard in my subway station. I stare at her face every morning while waiting for my train."

"Seriously?"

"Yeah. I mean, she's freaking gorgeous right? It's a nice sight when I'm trying to wake up before getting to work." Something seemed to click in Brian's head. "But she . . . and you . . ." His eyes widened and his voice dropped to a whisper. "Are you dating Gabrielle Levesque?"

Abby blushed and bit her lip. "By some definition of *dating*, I guess so. We've gone out a few times."

Brian was staring at her as though he'd never seen her before.

Abby swallowed around the heat in her cheeks and went to find Marcy to see if she could beg off an hour early. Knowing that Gabrielle was sitting somewhere in the shelves was going to be a distraction of the worst kind, and Abby knew she was going to be completely useless for the rest of the day.

When she found Gabrielle half an hour later, the other woman was curled up in an armchair with a fantasy novel.

"I haven't read that one before," she said, perching on the arm of the chair.

Gabrielle turned the page, then wrapped her arm around Abby's waist and tucked her fingers in the pocket of Abby's pants. "Let me finish this chapter?"

Abby smiled. She'd said those words a thousand times before to other people, so she was content to twirl her fingers through Gabrielle's hair and inhale the spicy perfume she was wearing until Gabrielle closed the book with a satisfied *thunk*.

"You can always check that out and finish it later," Abby said.

"I know how it ends," Gabrielle said, smiling up at her. "And I'd rather spend 'later' with you. Are you ready to go?"

Abby slid off the arm of the chair, and offered a hand to help Gabrielle up as well. She waited patiently while Gabrielle slid the book back on its shelf, and then Gabrielle was at her side again, twining their fingers together.

"Shall we?"

It was surreal to walk out of the library with Gabrielle next to her, waving goodbye to a still awe-struck Brian and stepping into the sunlight. She half expected people on the sidewalk to stop and stare, but no one seemed to notice the two women standing just a bit too close together.

"Will you take me back to your apartment?" Gabrielle asked.

The question cut through the dreamlike world that Abby had built up in her head. "It's . . . it won't be what you're used to," she said carefully.

Gabrielle looked at her, not slowing down. "How do you mean?"

"I mean . . . my apartment is small. Like, tiny. It's basically a shoebox, and I share it with a friend from college. It's nothing like the gorgeous condo you live in."

"Abigail, I don't care about apartments," Gabrielle said, stopping now to face her. "Not my own, and certainly not yours. I care about the person in the apartment with me, and right now I would like to be with you. At your home, or wherever you are comfortable."

Abby studied her, trying to determine if she was being sincere. It certainly seemed like Gabrielle was telling the truth. *And she didn't even look twice when she saw me in the library with rumpled clothes and no makeup.*

"Okay," Abby said. "Come on."

chapter

Seventeen

Standing on the crowded bus with Gabrielle was so surreal that it bordered on absurd. Surrounded by tired office workers, Gabrielle stood out like a sore thumb, and people did start to notice her in the confined space. Men did head-to-toe sweeps, and a few women frowned as though they recognized her but weren't sure from where.

Abby hit the button for her stop, and Gabrielle grabbed her hand and tugged her close before she could step off on her own. The gesture made Abby smile, and Gabrielle seemed pleased as they walked up the block to Abby's apartment.

"You've been warned," Abby said when they arrived, unlocking the door and pushing it open.

"Duly so," Gabrielle agreed, and stepped into the apartment without hesitation.

Abby tried to observe it through new eyes as she flipped on the lights. Did Gabrielle see how the couch was starting to fray on the edges, or the way shoes were piled up at the door where she and Jenna kicked them off upon walking in?

"It's lovely," Gabrielle said.

Abby snorted. "It's not too bad," she retorted.

"I lived in much worse, when I first got started as an actress," Gabrielle said. "It is clearly your home. You have pictures on the walls, movies displayed, books on every surface. It is very much a place that I can picture you living."

Abby wanted to ask about the first thing Gabrielle had mentioned, but it wasn't the time.

"Can I get you something to drink? We have water, soda, and

probably a box of wine, although it's definitely the cheap stuff."

Gabrielle shook her head and motioned for the couch. "Come sit with me," she said. "I would like to know what happened after Saturday."

Abby exhaled. "You must have an idea."

"Darren." Gabrielle spoke the word with certainty.

"And you," Abby added. If they were going to have this talk, she needed to be honest.

Gabrielle's eyes shut briefly. "Yes, and me. I have a reputation, and it is one that I've unfortunately earned."

"They call you the Ice Queen," Abby whispered.

"Yes."

Abby studied Gabrielle. "I couldn't figure out why at first," she said. "When we met, even at the restaurant, you were a bit distant but never cruel like everyone warned me you would be."

That seemed to surprise Gabrielle. "They warned you about me?"

"They said you would hurt me."

Gabrielle accepted that with a frown.

"And then the night at your apartment, when Darren showed up, I think that was the first time I'd seen the Ice Queen in action."

Gabrielle's smile lacked any trace of humor. "Yes, Darren does tend to bring out the worst in me."

Abby couldn't hold the question back. "Are you sleeping with him?"

Gabrielle's eyes went wide.

"I mean, it's okay if you are. We haven't—we aren't dating, I guess," Abby added hurriedly.

"Did he say that we are?"

Abby's heart sank. *Avoidance.* "He definitely implied it," she said. "So it's true?"

"No." Gabrielle spit the word out. "I am not sleeping with him."

"But you were."

Gabrielle's fire went out, and she looked tired suddenly. "Yes." She sighed and looked away. "I used to. We were lovers when I first came to New York. He was my manager when I began getting roles on Broadway. At one point I thought I loved him."

"What happened?"

But Gabrielle shook her head. "That story is for another time."

Abby bit back a frustrated sigh. She'd thought Gabrielle was finally opening up, but as she watched the other woman closed off before her eyes. "Tell me something else then," she said. "Tell me about leaving home? You said you lived in an apartment smaller than this one."

Gabrielle turned back to Abby, tucking her legs up on the couch next to her and curling her body into Abby's. Her face was hidden against Abby's neck now, warm breath raising goosebumps along Abby's arm. "You do ask the difficult questions, Abigail."

"Sorry," Abby mumbled.

"No, it's okay." Gabrielle seemed to be thinking. "I would like to tell you these things, but it is not easy. The last time I trusted someone enough to open up to them . . ."

Realization hit Abby all at once, a lightning bold jolting through her. Gabrielle admitting, *"I thought I loved him"*, and the look on her face when she talked about Darren. His jealousy, manipulation and anger.

She wanted to badly to ask, to get confirmation, but Gabrielle seemed so wary of giving her trust again.

But Abby was pretty damned sure that Darren had used Gabrielle's trust and betrayed it in some way. Why she was still stuck with him as a manager was incomprehensible.

"I wanted to be on stage from a very young age," Gabrielle said. "Growing up in Quebec was . . . not easy. My mother died when I was young, and my father was very cold, bitter. He saw much of my mother in me, I think, and it hurt him. I escaped into books a lot growing up, and in watching musicals on tape. As soon I was old enough, I used what little savings I had to move to Toronto, rent a tiny closet of an apartment, and audition for the Performing Arts school there."

It was possibly the longest speech Abby had ever heard Gabrielle make.

"You got in," she said.

She could feel Gabrielle smile against her neck. "Yes. And I excelled."

"So why don't you act anymore?"

But Gabrielle just pressed a kiss to Abby's neck instead of

answering. Abby sighed, tilting her head to the side to allow more access. *I guess sharing time is over for now.*

"I am glad you didn't send me away when I showed up at the library today," Gabrielle said. "I was worried you were upset, and that you were planning to end our relationship."

Abby felt a rush of guilt, because hadn't she been debating whether or not to do that very thing over the last few days? Her mother and Sara had told her to give the relationship another chance, so when Gabrielle had appeared she'd already been planning to do just that.

"I'm glad you came to see me," she said truthfully.

When Gabrielle pulled away, Abby turned, and then they were kissing, Gabrielle pressing against her so tenderly that for the first few breaths it felt like a piece of silk brushing against her lips, a whisper of softness and nothing more. Gabrielle tentatively moved closer, pressing against Abby's mouth as though treasuring something valuable, worshiping.

Abby had kissed passionately before, had kissed until she was out of breath, but this was a level of intimacy that made her heart pound against her chest as though it were trying to escape.

Gabrielle's hands pulled gently at Abby until she turned her body on the couch to face Gabrielle, and the better angle allowed Gabrielle to slip in deeper, working her way beneath Abby's skin with a slow increase of pressure against her lips and her waist.

When Gabrielle pulled away for a moment to catch her breath, her eyes were blown wide, the brown almost obscured.

Warm fingers found the thin gap between Abby's work shirt and pants, and teased at the hint of skin that was bared when Abby twisted in for another kiss. Abby squirmed away from the touch, a burst of laughter escaping against Gabrielle's mouth.

"You're ticklish." Gabrielle said.

Abby didn't have time to respond before the fingers were back, this time settling against the spot on her side more firmly. She met Gabrielle's gaze and found those dark eyes filled with amusement, and had a second to brace herself before Gabrielle descended.

She screeched.

Gabrielle twisted over her, finding the ticklish points on her stomach, the back of her knee, the side of her neck, and Abby squirmed beneath her, trying to escape back into the couch until Gabrielle was looming over her.

They were both laughing by the time Abby shouted for mercy and Gabrielle finally allowed her a reprieve. Abby's chest ached, her cheeks sore from smiling so widely, and Gabrielle was afire with red cheeks and eyes that shone.

"You look so happy right now," Abby whispered as she tried to catch her breath.

Gabrielle leaned over, her long hair creating a private room just for the two of them, blocking off the rest of the world so Gabrielle could lean in and kiss her again, and again.

"I'm so glad you came here," Abby said, echoing her earlier statement. "After Saturday I wasn't sure what to think, if I even wanted to see you anymore. But this is the most perfect apology I can imagine."

Gabrielle got a strange look on her face. "Then let me apologize," she said, leaning forward. The kiss this time had a different emotion behind it. The easy intimacy and comfort was gone, replaced by a fierce passion. Gabrielle seemed to flip a switch, using her tongue and teeth until Abby's lips were swollen, hands changing from playful to seductive as they slid down Abby's side and once again found the edge of her shirt. This time, though, they widened the gap of skin there, pushing Abby's shirt up her stomach.

Gabrielle's lips vanished from her own, and the weight above her shifted until Gabrielle's mouth had found a new target: the skin of Abby's lower stomach, pressing kisses to the warm skin there.

"Gabrielle," Abby said, and her voice sounded weak, uneasy.

Gabrielle's fingers found the button of her work pants.

"Not like this," Abby said. "I don't want you to apologize to me like this."

Gabrielle froze, and Abby held her breath.

"I don't understand," Gabrielle finally said, refusing to meet Abby's gaze.

Abby let out the breath that she'd been holding. "You wanted to apologize," she said, "but I don't want you to apologize with sex. I'm not . . ." She bit her tongue, trapping the words against the back of her teeth.

Gabrielle slumped against her, face turned to the side, body going soft. Was she disappointed? She breathed against Abby's body until Abby thought she might have fallen asleep. Then she pushed herself up, hair tumbling around her and clothing rumpled. She gave Abby a long, steady look, and then nodded as though she'd made a decision.

"Okay."

"Really?" Abby asked incredulously.

She got a smile from Gabrielle, tentative at first before turning warm. "Yes, okay" she said. "Another time then."

Abby gave a wavering smile in return, and her stomach sank. Of course, Gabrielle still anticipated sex in their relationship. Maybe she thought Abby was shy, or that she just genuinely wasn't in the mood right then, but eventually she would expect sex.

Gabrielle didn't give her time to linger on the sobering thought; she slid back up the couch, wrapping herself around Abby, shuffling them until they were lying on the couch face to face, breath mingling as their racing hearts slowed down.

"I will make this right," she said.

"It's alright now"

Gabrielle hummed. "Let's re-write the last two dates. This weekend we can go to the food festival. I have no plans on Sunday, and will make sure that does not change. And the following Friday night I hope you'll come back to my apartment for dinner, and this time I will ensure there are no interruptions."

Abby gave her a radiant smile. "That sounds perfect."

They traded lazy kisses, and Abby soaked up the heat of another body surrounding her own, until her empty stomach starting to protest. Gabrielle laughed at her, finally opening her arms to let them both sit back up.

"I should go," Gabrielle said. "You need to eat and rest. You work tomorrow?"

Abby grimaced and looked down. "Yeah."

Gabrielle touched her shoulder. "I am sorry if I got you in any trouble by showing up at your work today."

"No, it's not a problem!" Abby exclaimed. "I mean, I'll get teased all day tomorrow by Brian, but he has a pretty intense crush on you from what I saw, so I'm sure it'll be playful jealousy." She paused. *Do I tell her?* Gabrielle had been honest with her, had opened up, so it was only fair that Abby return the gesture. "It's work itself."

"I thought you loved working at the library."

"I did. I do." Abby sighed, her eyes falling shut. "They're closing our branch down in a month. We got the final confirmation this morning, and I managed to forget about it once you showed up. But tomorrow is going to be rough."

Gabrielle brushed a kiss across her cheek. "Oh, *mon lapin*, I am so sorry." She seemed genuinely saddened by the news, drawing Abby in close.

"I'm going to try to transfer to another branch," Abby said, letting herself be comforted. So far everyone had been angry and stressed like Brian and Marcy, or worried like Jenna, or just frustratingly unhelpful like her mother. To be held and shown sympathy was something new, and Abby melted into it.

But Gabrielle pulled back. "Then I will do everything I can to help you keep your mind occupied until you are able to find a new position elsewhere," she said firmly.

This is the Ice Queen that everyone warned me about? Abby leaned in to bury her face in Gabrielle's neck and whisper her thanks against the skin there. *They were wrong.*

chapter

Eighteen

"I think I'm falling in love."

Sara jerked her head up, eyes round. "Seriously?"

Nathan sighed dreamily. "Yeah."

Abby laughed at the consternation on Sara's face. "He's not that bad looking," she said.

"You too, Abs?" Sara flopped back against the couch. "I'm sorry, I just don't see it. Besides, Abby, you're dating a freakin' model. Like, how do you go from her to . . . that?" she gestured at the screen in front of them and the object of their discussion.

"It's the voice," Nathan explained.

"And the way he moves," Abby added.

"You're both seriously crazy," Sara said. She pulled out her phone and fired off a quick text.

Nathan peeked over her shoulder as she hit Send, then scrabbled to grab the phone from her. "You can't send that!"

"Too late!" Sara grinned gleefully. She caught Abby's confused expression and winked. "I just let Jason know that he's been replaced by a hook-nosed potions professor with greasy hair."

Nathan crossed his arms. "Whatever, I keep catching Jason watching that singing reality show because he thinks the judge is ridiculously hot." He kicked his feet up and turned his attention back to the screen. "It's been way too long since I watched these movies. Great suggestion Abby!"

Abby was curled up on the end of the couch, hugging a pillow. "Gabrielle loves them," she said. "We were talking about them over text yesterday, and I had the urge to watch them again."

"I am always happy to host a movie marathon." Sara looked into the bowl of popcorn and sighed forlornly. "But I call not-it on making another bowl before the third movie starts."

While Sara and Nathan descended back into friendly bickering, Abby rolled off the couch to stretch, grabbing the popcorn bowl and working out kinks in her neck as she wandered into the kitchen. It was already eleven o'clock at night, and even though it was Saturday her body was telling her it was long past her bedtime.

"I can only watch one more before I need to head home," she called, fishing a bag of popcorn from the box on the counter and tossing it in the microwave. The thought of her Sunday plans made her smile, cock her hip against the counter and tug out her phone while she waited for the microwave to do its thing.

She and Gabrielle were meeting at noon to walk the food festival, and Gabrielle had been texting her all evening to talk about how excited she was.

"Speaking of being in love," Nathan said, wandering into the kitchen and making a beeline for the fridge. "That look on your face is giving me diabetes."

"Hush," Abby said, not glancing up from the message she was sending about their actor debate. She hit Send and tucked the phone back away as the microwave dinged. Nathan's words caught up with her and she added, "And I'm not in love yet."

Nathan grabbed a can of soda from the fridge. "Yet," he said, popping the tab on it.

Abby focused on pouring the popcorn into the bowl. When she turned with the steaming popcorn, however, Nathan was waiting. She sighed. "Yeah, not yet. But . . . I could be? I think I could be."

"You've only known her for two months," Nathan pointed out. "And your dates have been pretty underwhelming, from what I hear."

Abby let the heat from the bowl seep into her palms, using it to ground her. "The very first time I saw her, my breath caught in my chest," she said. "But then on the first date, I realized that there was something more to her than a beautiful woman whose emotions were impossible to crack."

Nathan waited silently, the sound of the movie in the background a comforting white noise.

"You know those pictures of icebergs?" Abby asked.

He nodded.

"The top, what we can see above the water, is magnificent and dangerous. But it's only a small fraction of what's hiding beneath the surface, and it leaves us awe-struck when we see the entire picture. That's Gabrielle."

"A sharp block of ice?" Nathan asked, quirking an eyebrow to take the sting out of the question.

Abby laughed. "Cold and imposing where the world sees her," she said, "but with so much depth if you just take the time to look beneath. I'm still getting a clear picture of the entire woman, but each time I see more it's confirmation that she's someone I want to be with."

Sara called to them, asking where her popcorn was. Abby started to head back into the living room, but Nathan stopped her with a hand on her arm.

"Have you told her that you're ace?" he asked.

Abby shook her head. "Not yet. I'm . . . afraid. I've just found her, and I don't' want to lose her."

She was thankful when Nathan just pursed his lips and nodded.

The next morning was overcast and a bit cool for late May, but the forecast wasn't calling for rain when Abby dragged her tired body from bed and found half a pot of coffee waiting for her on the kitchen counter. "God bless you, Jenna," she mumbled, pouring a cup. It had been almost two before she'd gotten home that morning, and she was due to meet Gabrielle in a couple of hours.

She stared at her closet while sipping her coffee, trying to figure out what to wear.

"Okay, this shouldn't be so hard." She scolded herself, one hand on her hip. "She didn't even notice when she saw you in the library looking like a mess."

"Talking to yourself is a sure sign of insanity," Jenna said from her doorway.

Abby jumped and spilled coffee on her hand. "Ow, shit," she said, switching the mug to her other hand and shaking the sting out.

Jenna vanished to the kitchen and returned with a paper towel, passing it over. "Didn't mean to scare you," she said. "I just heard you moving around and wanted to stick my head in and see how the job search was going."

Any chance of a good mood forming that morning vanished. "It's going," Abby lied through her teeth. "I've talked with a few other branches, so I'm sure I'll be able to transfer over in a few weeks with no problem."

She *had* spoken with various branches in the area, but the truth was that none of them were hiring. Budget cuts were hitting everyone, and other libraries were looking at cutting staff and hours as well. But the relief on Jenna's face helped to soothe the queasy feeling that the lie left in Abby's stomach.

"Awesome, I'm keeping my fingers crossed for you," Jenna said. "So what are you up to today?"

"Heading to Smorgasburg," Abby said, welcoming the change of topic.

Jenna's eyes lit up. "I haven't been yet this year," she said. "Got room for one more?"

"Ahhh . . ." Abby blushed. "It's actually a date?"

Jenna backed down immediately. "Say no more," she said, holding her hands up and giving Abby a grin. "You're still seeing the mysterious beau who sent the roses?"

"Yeah." Abby turned back to her closet. She pulled out her favorite jeans, comfortable and hugging all the right places, and a green and blue button-down that she could roll the sleeves up on.

"You're getting serious about this one, aren't you?" Jenna leaned against the doorframe, watching Abby set the clothes out on her bed. "It's been a few months, and I don't think I've ever seen you go on more than a few dates with anyone in the past."

Abby dug out a pair of sneakers as well. "Yeah, I think so. I *hope* so."

Jenna saluted her with her own cup of coffee. "Well best of luck to you and your mystery lover." She turned to head out the door, calling over her shoulder, "And let me know how the food festival is!"

Abby finished getting dressed, enjoying the feeling of comfortable clothes for once. She brushed her hair out, twisting it up into a messy bun on top of her head, and found her lip gloss.

"This is me," she said to the mirror. "If Gabrielle can begin to show me the real her, I can definitely do the same."

She took the train out to Prospect Park, emerging from the underground to find Gabrielle leaning elegantly against the fence at the park entrance. She was wearing dark jeans that probably cost more than one of Abby's paychecks, and a white blouse that made her skin glow in the faint sunlight. Gabrielle spotted her immediately and gave her a wide smile as Abby crossed the street.

"Abigail." She leaned forward, as though she was going to brush a kiss on her cheek, but instead she cupped Abby's face and gave her a quick, dirty kiss. "I've missed you."

Abby returned the kiss, blushing furiously when a couple of college boys whistled. She leaned back on her heels, but Gabrielle didn't let her get too far, taking her hand and leading her into the park.

They followed the crowd of people and the smell of food until dozens and dozens of tents appeared.

Gabrielle was looking around in wonder as they passed , clearly delighted, and Abby found the excitement to be contagious. She pushed her the lingering worry from her conversation with Jenna, and focused on Gabrielle and their date instead.

"How was your week?" Abby asked as they weaved through the lines and groups of people.

"It was fine."

Abby paused, tugging Gabrielle to stop with her. "Which means it wasn't fine." This was one of the things that she'd learned quickly about Gabrielle: when something was upsetting to her, she shut down.

Gabrielle hesitated, then continued to walk, leaving Abby no choice but to follow. "It was not a good week," she said. "I find that my ability to handle difficult situations is not the best to begin with."

Abby rolled her eyes. "Babe, you are the master of understatement."

Instead of being offended, Gabrielle just laughed. "Yes, I suspect you're right." She squeezed Abby's hand. "I like that. Babe. I've never had a nickname before, or a lover's name."

The question was on the tip of Abby's tongue. *Darren never called you anything sweet? No terms of endearment?* But she didn't want to bring up Darren, not when Gabrielle was relaxed and smiling. "You should have a nickname. Gabrielle is a bit long to say when I'm whispering in your ear."

"Unfortunately, the obvious nickname is one that I do not particularly enjoy."

"Yeah, you're not exactly a Gabby," she said. "Plus, Gabby and Abby sounds like a tween Disney Channel show."

Gabrielle grimaced and then grinned. "Yes, I agree."

They kept walking for a minute, before Abby spotted a sign on one of the food vendors. "I have it!" She grinned at Gabrielle. "Brie."

"Like the cheese?".

"Sure, like the cheese," Abby agreed. "Soft, creamy. French."

Gabrielle didn't look convinced. "I'm not French," she pointed out.

Abby tilted her head, conceding. "Fair enough." Her mind was working quickly. "But, much like brie-the-cheese, you would make an excellent dessert."

Gabrielle did laugh now, tilting her head back. "Okay, you've convinced me," she said. "But only if we can stop and have one of these ham and brie biscuits, because now I'm hungry!"

They joined the line, both of them still trading smiles, and it wasn't until Gabrielle had handed her a biscuit that Abby realized the other woman had expertly deflected from her original question.

Good try, Brie, but I'm not giving up yet. "Tell me about this week," she prompted again.

Gabrielle took a small bite of her food, chewing slowly. "I do not want to keep modeling," she said firmly.

"Then quit."

"It's not so easy," Gabrielle said. "I'm under contract, and Darren . . ."

So it was Gabrielle who was going to bring up the angry elephant in the room. "He's forcing you?" she asked.

"Not so obviously." Gabrielle exhaled, shaking her head. "He is much more sly about it. He will arrange a meeting with a designer or photographer without letting me know, and then I cannot say no after or I will be seen negatively by others."

The words were simple, spoken with little emotion, and made it immediately obvious how Gabrielle had been twisted and trapped. "Very Slytherin," Abby said.

Gabrielle smiled ever so slightly at that, but it didn't reach her eyes.

"Can you take him to court and break your contract?" Abby asked.

That got her another sigh. "The idea is one that I have considered many times," Gabrielle said. "But there is much more to it than a lawsuit. Darren is cunning, and he has made sure to trap me in a web that I cannot easily escape."

"How?"

Gabrielle appeared deep in thought, her gaze distant as they walked slowly through the crowds of people. Eventually she spoke. "I told him something once, in confidence. A secret that I trusted him with, about my father. He used that secret against me to get me to accept a lucrative modeling contract that I had already informed him I was not interested in, and he manipulated me to the point where I had no choice but to continue in modeling after."

It was unimaginable to Abby, that someone could do something so cruel. "Why would he do that, though? I don't understand. And you could still leave him."

Gabrielle's sigh was filled with sadness. "To do so could mean the end for my career. Darren has made sure to burn the bridges I left behind in the theater community; I did not make him enough money there, and modeling is much more lucrative. So I cannot go back, but going forward is also impossible."

Money. It explained everything; Darren had gotten greedy, and Gabrielle was trapped and miserable as a result. Abby stepped closer to her, so their arms brushed against each other with every step. "He would trash your name in the modeling community, so you wouldn't be able to get work there."

"Yes." Gabrielle grimaced. "And my father would . . ."

They continued walking, a bubble of somber silence in the crowd. Abby wanted to ask the questions that piled up on her tongue. When they'd had dinner at Gabrielle's apartment, Brie had told her about her father's cruelty, and the way she'd escaped into books and, later, acting as a result. But there was clearly more to the story than that. Abby wasn't sure if she wanted to know this part of the story, though; anything that put such sadness and despair on Gabrielle's face was best skipped over.

"Okay, tell me something good that happened this week," Abby said, trying a different topic.

She let Gabrielle tell her about the play she'd managed to see that Tuesday night, taking advantage of an appointment Darren had arranged that had been cancelled at the last minute. Abby watched Gabrielle as she spoke, the way she lit up when talking about the acting and costumes.

They stopped at a booth selling small chocolate truffles, and Abby's mouth was watering when she took a bite, eyes fluttering shut as flavor exploded on her tongue. When she opened them again, Gabrielle had stopped speaking and was staring, eyes hungry, thoughher gaze was fixed firmly on Abigail.

"Sorry," Abby said.

"For that, you do not *ever* need to apologize," Gabrielle said seriously.

Abby offered the small paper tray of chocolates to Gabrielle, who declined.

"I would never eat chocolate again, if it meant getting to see that look on your face every time you did."

Abby blushed, delighted.

Gabrielle leaned over, right there in the middle of the crowds, and kissed her once, twice, tongue darting out to catch a tiny bit of chocolate that Abby had missed. "Thank you for today."

Yeah, Abby thought, giving Gabrielle another kiss, *I am definitely starting to fall in love. This is going to hurt so much when it finally comes crashing down around me.*

chapter

Nineteen

The world was conspiring against Abby.

At least, she was pretty sure that whatever deity might have been up there was having a great laugh at her expense that week.

Monday started off as all Mondays did: miserably, with Abby yawning as she crawled out of bed and into the shower. She contemplated stopping at one of the coffee shops near her apartment, but winced at the thought of spending five bucks on a cup of joe and made a pot of instant instead

She poured the coffee into a travel mug, grabbed her bag, and headed down the steps and out the door. Only to stop dead as a wall of water met her.

"Well damn." It was pouring, which she'd somehow managed to miss in her half-awake state. She had to duck back inside for an umbrella, and then managed to get soaked anyways as she waited for the bus.

Things did not improve from there.

On Tuesday Jenna announced that she was having a few friends in from out of town who would be crashing in their living room over the weekend. The idea of complete strangers invading their apartment was not an appealing one, but a little voice in the back of her head reminded her that she still hadn't found a job and it might not be her apartment to share for much longer anyway.

Wednesday was the day Brian finally gave in to his curiosity and perched on a chair next to Abby during a morning break.

"So."

Abby eyed him wearily. "So?"

"Gabrielle Levesque."

Abby sighed. "Yes, Gabrielle Levesque."

Brian propped his chin on his hands, leaning forward. "I've been trying to figure this out for four days, and I can't get it to compute in my head. How'd you meet? Isn't she . . . I don't know, really mean? That's what the tabloids all say."

So instead of enjoying an apple and kicking her feet up on her mid-morning break, Abby found herself sharing vague details of how they'd met and how Gabrielle was actually incredibly sweet. "The person that the media sees isn't who she truly is," Abby said.

"Have you met any other famous people while hanging out with her?"

Abby rolled her eyes. "Okay, you've had your fill of my private life," she said. "Let me spend the last few minutes of my break in peace and quiet."

Brian eased up, but the questions kept coming for the rest of the day.

On Thursday, she was supposed to meet up with Sara and Nathan, but Sara had a cold and Jason had apparently surprised him with tickets to a baseball game, so she found herself moping around the apartment.

And on Friday, she got an email from her mother with a link.

"Mom, what's this?" Abby tucked the phone against her ear, staring at the email on her computer.

"Well, I thought it might be interesting for you to read," her mother said.

Abby tugged on her hair, counting backwards from ten silently before speaking. "How did you even *find* this?" she asked. "You know what, wait. Don't answer that."

She'd clicked the link without thinking, and then promptly closed the page out when she'd read the headline.

"Abigail, you were worried about keeping that woman of yours, right? This could help." Her mother was using that voice that said, *Look, I have done a thing to help you so you'd better accept it with gratitude.* "I didn't *read* it or anything, just saw the subject."

Yeah, the subject: TEN WAYS TO PLEASURE YOUR GIRLFRIEND.

"Mom, I don't need this," Abby said. *I don't* want *this.* "Thanks for thinking of me, but I don't need links like this."

But the article lingered at the back of her mind for the rest of the day. She was meeting Gabrielle for dinner that night at her apartment, and she kept recalling what her mother had said, what the article suggested, what society in general seemed to accept as mandatory in a relationship.

Gabrielle would want to have sex. Probably tonight. But while Abby was becoming more and more certain that she wanted a relationship with Brie, she didn't know how to give her that. Abby knew what people had said about her in the past: that she was frigid, weird, broken. That not wanting to have sex made her somehow less than human. And despite that she'd accepted her asexuality for what it was, never mourned the loss of something she didn't want in the first place.

But she didn't want to lose Gabrielle.

She left the library, still thinking about the article.

She got home and stripped off her work clothes, and couldn't stop thinking about the article.

She found her nicest pair of jeans and a silky top that she wore when she went out sometimes. She slipped on a pair of sandals, tugged on a jacket to ward off the last hints of winter that lingered late at night. She put on makeup.

She kept thinking about the article.

On the train ride into Manhattan, she pulled the link back up on her phone, tilting it so no one could read over her shoulder. She read the entire page, first with clinical detachment and then with a strange curiosity that was equal parts *why would anyone want to do that?* and *how does that even work?*

When she did slide her phone back into her back pocket, there was a sinking feeling in her stomach.

Could she do the things on that list? Sure. Did she want to? Yeah, if it was what Gabrielle wanted. Her parents had always said that relationships were about compromise, and this was probably a compromise she could make.

Would Gabrielle compromise with her in return?

The conductor announced her stop over the scratchy speaker, and Abby grabbed the railing as she stood, feeling off-balance in more ways than one.

Gabrielle met her at the door with a smile and a kiss, and Abby could physically see the stiffness of the day dissolving from her shoulders when she wrapped her arms around Abby.

"Come in," Gabrielle said, opening the door. "I assure you tonight there will be no interruptions. I've told Darren that I am out with friends this evening, and have convinced a few people to mention so on social media. He will not come here searching for me."

"That's a relief," Abby said. She followed Gabrielle into the apartment, watching as the other woman used her hands to talk animatedly about the food that would be delivered soon.

Gabrielle caught her watching and raised an eyebrow in question.

"You look so relaxed right now," Abby explained. "I feel like the more I see you lately, the more you unwind."

"There's an obvious correlation there," Gabrielle pointed out. "I enjoy your company. I enjoy being with you. I can trust you."

Abby stopped at that. "You trust me?"

Gabrielle shrugged gracefully. "I do."

But Abby could read the tense lines beneath the movement, and knew it wasn't so simple. Gabrielle had told her how she'd been in a relationship before and had her trust ripped away, how she didn't trust anymore.

"That means a lot to me, Brie," she said, using the nickname they'd created at the food festival.

As she'd intended, Gabrielle smiled at it. "I hope you will trust me in return someday."

"Trust you with what?"

"To not hurt you."

Abby did trust Gabrielle, as much as she trusted anyone really. But there was still a possibility Gabrielle could—and would—hurt her. Whether through another visit from the Ice Queen or her manager getting between them, or if (when) Gabrielle left her because Abby couldn't give her the relationship she needed.

Her mind could picture a million different scenarios. Gabrielle going back to Darren, or finding another lover. Darren's manipulations pulling Gabrielle away until they never had any time to see each other. Gabrielle's coldness and cruelty turning her on Abby someday.

Gabrielle must have picked up on some of what Abby was thinking, because she smiled sadly. "Someday." She changing the subject back to the food delivery, her voice cheerful, though Abby thought the mood was a bit forced. "I believe dinner will be here soon. Help me set the table?"

Abby pulled down plates and glasses while Gabrielle found a bottle of wine and silverware, and tried not to let her thoughts consume her. By the time the door buzzed with their dinner, she'd managed to push them away, and was smiling as Gabrielle brought in two bags from an upscale restaurant that Abby recognized.

"Okay, tell me about the plan for tonight."

They ate chicken marsala and linguine, and Abby let herself relax again, mimicking Gabrielle's easy smile and comfort. Gabrielle told her about a movie she wanted to put on, a science fiction drama that she'd missed when it was in theaters.

They carefully managed to avoid the topics neither of them wanted to bring up: Gabrielle's manager and Abby's job.

"Tell me a story," Gabrielle said, when the conversation died down for a moment.

Abby's eyebrows furrowed. "What kind of story?"

Gabrielle twirled strands of pasta around her fork. "Something you've seen, or someone you've met," she said. "I remember you telling me that you enjoy coming up with stories about the people you encounter, so maybe tell me one of their stories."

It was an odd request, but one that made Abby smile. "I'm surprised you remember that."

"You said you wanted to know my story," Gabrielle said, as though that were explanation enough.

"I also said that I thought you were fascinating," Abby reminded her. She got a satisfying flush of red on Gabrielle's cheeks. "You denied it then, but I haven't changed my mind yet."

"And I still believe you are mistaken. The fascinating one is you, Abigail, with your marvelous way of seeing the world. So tell me a story. Fascinate me."

Abby's cheeks grew hot, but she launched into a story about two older women who had come in a few days before, holding hands and looking peaceful together with their matching gray hair and wrinkled smiles. They'd browsed the aisles for a while, asked for assistance to look up a book on the computer, and had finally checked out a couple of mystery novels. "In my head, they've been together since before it was safe to be together," she said. "They've weathered political storms, family and society judging them, and remained together the whole time." The fantasy spun out in her head, and Abby couldn't help but smile wistfully.

"I would like that someday," Gabrielle said. "Someone to be with for the rest of my life."

"Someone to hold hands with even when the world seems against you," Abby agreed.

"Yes, exactly." Gabrielle looked at her as she said the words.

That could be you. Gabrielle was the woman she could see herself holding hands with as they explored bookstores and went to the theater. She had a feeling that she'd never grow bored with Gabrielle, always learning more about her.

They finished dinner and moved into the living room. This time when they sat on the couch to watch the movie, Abby let Gabrielle curl up beside her, wrapping an arm around Gabrielle's waist and lacing their fingers together over her stomach.

She'd assumed they would talk during the movie, maybe trade kisses while pretending to pay attention, but at first they just sat in comfortable silence, punctuated by gasps and laughter as the action unfolded.

Halfway through the movie, Gabrielle got up get a bottle of water. When she hadn't come back after several minutes, Abby paused the movie and went to follow.

She found Gabrielle standing at the fridge, staring at a photo that was stuck on it with a magnet.

"I didn't expect you to be a pictures-on-the-fridge type of person," Abby said.

Gabrielle startled. "Abigail, sorry," she said. "I got lost in my own thoughts."

Abby approached and hooked her chin over Gabrielle's shoulder, looking at the picture with her. She hadn't paid attention to these little details of Gabrielle's life yet, and wasn't expecting the picture she saw.

Gabrielle, smiling, with two men on either side of her. One of them was fair-skinned with dark hair, but he had Gabrielle's nose and eyes and was standing slightly away from her. He was thin and pale, the kind that said *illness* and not genetics. The other man in the picture, his hand wrapped around Gabrielle's waist and chin tilted up as he grinned at the camera, was Darren.

"I don't know why I keep this picture," Gabrielle said. "Maybe to remind myself of what I have achieved, and what I have left behind."

Abby massaged her other shoulder soothingly. "That's your dad, isn't it?"

"Yes. Darren invited my father to see me here in New York. He flew him out, got him a hotel room." She paused, laughing humorlessly. "It was not a pleasant surprise."

Abby didn't want to talk about Darren, but she wanted to know more about Abby's family. "You never talk about him," Abby said, tapping on her dad.

"That's because we do not talk. He lives in Montreal, and I have not seen him in several years." She paused. "He is very sick. Cancer. It was discovered shortly before this picture was taken, but he went into remission. Two years later, the cancer came back."

Abby turned Gabrielle around. "Hey." She leaned up to kiss her gently. "You must see that picture half a dozen times a day. What's on your mind right now that it's suddenly bothering you?"

Gabrielle leaned into the gesture like she was touch-starved, and Abby brushed a thumb over her cheekbones, reveling in the soft skin there. "I told Darren about the cancer shortly after I found out. We had been dating for almost a year at that point. Even then I was not close to my father, but the diagnosis... it terrified me. So I turned to Darren, hoping for comfort. And I told him that my father had asked for money to cover treatment. In Canada, the healthcare will pay for the treatment itself, but he would still have the house, his car payments, food to purchase. And he would be unable to work, he said. I could help him, but the money would be tight."

Abby looked over Gabrielle's shoulders to the picture, and the way she was smiling with Darren's arm around her. "What happened?"

"Darren invited my father to see me. He announced over dinner that the two of us would be happy to write him a check, to help him with his financial trouble."

"He didn't ask you before deciding that."

"No." Gabrielle looked away, eyes unfocused.

Abby could see the story unfolding in her head. The way Darren would have manipulated her, positioned her so she couldn't possibly say otherwise without destroying what remained of her relationship with her father.

"But if you didn't have the money . . ." Abby frowned, her hand finding Gabrielle's shoulder to rub gentle circles into the tense muscles she found there.

"Ah." Gabrielle smiled sadly. "But remember, I had been offered a modeling contract that I had turned down. One that offered more money than any Broadway role I had ever signed."

"He made you sign it."

Gabrielle leaned into Abby's touch, though she didn't relax. "He was very convincing. He said I would be foolish to turn down such a lucrative contract when doing so would allow my father to heal and live comfortably. It would be selfish." She shuddered. "I signed the contract that he put before me. And I hated every second of that first modelling job. But at the time, I thought *what choice do I have?*"

Abby exhaled. "And then he destroyed any chance you might have of going back to theater after that."

"Yes."

Abby tried to imagine what Gabrielle must have felt: the betrayal, at having someone she trusted do something so thoughtlessly cruel. For money.

"I'm here," she said, resting her forehead against Gabrielle's. "For as long as you'll have me."

Gabrielle kissed her, something desperate in the action. Abby opened to her, letting her ground them both to reality.

"Come with me?" Gabrielle leaned back just enough to speak the words against Abby's mouth.

"Anywhere."

Gabrielle led her down the hallway, past the paused television and into a room Abby hadn't seen before.

Her bedroom.

Abby swallowed. She thought about the article. Thought about Gabrielle, and the reassurance that she was seeking.

I can do this. For her. I can give her what she needs.

Gabrielle tried to pull at the silky shirt Abby was wearing, but Abby stilled her hands. "No," she said softly. "Let me."

She stripped Gabrielle's clothes off, brushing her hand over her shoulder, ribs, hip as she did.

"Gabrielle," she murmured. "Brie. Let me do this for you."

Gabrielle surrendered, and Abby brought her to the point where she could stop thinking and simply trust with her body. She sought out the parts of Gabrielle's body that made her sigh, made her arch up, made her melt boneless into the mattress.

Abby treated it as a puzzle, a story unfolding. And when Gabrielle tensed and moaned, Abby found the conclusion, leaning up to kiss her gently, finding comfort in the softness in Gabrielle's gaze, the sleepy adoration.

Gabrielle fumbled with Abby's shirt again. "Let me pay you back."

"It's okay," Abby said. "This was for you."

Gabrielle's eyebrows drew together in confusion. "But you didn't get anything out of it."

Abby kissed her until the confused lines on her forehead eased. "I got everything that I needed to get," she said. "Rest here, I'm going to the bathroom for a second, and then I'll come curl up with you.

Standing in the bathroom, washing her hands and staring at her reflection, Abby tried to process the emotions coursing through her. She wasn't disgusted, she realized. She wasn't upset, at least not with Gabrielle or the situation. Instead, she was upset with herself.

I need to tell her. She looked out at the bed, Gabrielle curled up and sated in bed with her eyes closed. She made a whispered vow to her reflection. "I'll tell her. Soon."

She could be okay with this, if this was what Gabrielle needed. But she couldn't be okay with herself if she didn't tell Gabrielle the truth.

chapter

Twenty

A bby was waiting for Nathan when he arrived, sitting at a table in the hole-in-the-wall Thai restaurant that he'd texted her about. "You're early."

Abby glanced up from her menu, smiling, but was taken aback when she spotted Jason standing with him. She hadn't met the older man very often, and he was intimidating in the same was Gabrielle had been at first. He carried his wealth with the confidence of someone who had been born to it, and he was wearing a suit that was clearly tailored to his body, making him seem even more imposing. But the way he kept looking at Nathan—as though he never wanted to let him out of his sight—and the genuine smile he gave her, helped Abby relax.

"I told him I was meeting you here, and he all-but begged to come along," Nathan said, sliding into a chair and grinning as Jason pulled off his suit jacket and rolled his sleeves up, sitting beside him so they were shoulder to shoulder.

"You didn't mention you were meeting a friend," Jason said. "You just teased me that you were getting Thai without me, while I was stuck at home alone."

"Mean," Abby pointed out. "It's okay, Nate said this was one of your favorite restaurants."

Nathan grinned at both of them. He bumped his arm again Jason's playfully, then turned to Abby. "I'm sorry if you wanted to talk in private," he said. "We can get dessert after if you want, just the two of us."

Abby shook her head. "It's totally alright." She'd called Nathan to ask for a favor of sorts, but there wasn't anything especially confidential about it.

They ordered drinks and spring rolls, then Nathan propped his elbows up on the table. "So, what did you want to talk about?"

"How bad is Gabrielle's reputation in the theater community?" she asked without preamble.

Nathan sat back, clearly not expecting that question, and let out a low whistle. "I mean, it's not great," he said. "The rumor is that she'd auditioned for and been given a starring role in a major play, and then backed out before the contract was signed and never even bothered to call the directors . . . she had her manager send a nasty email on her behalf saying she'd found a better option. Upset a lot of people, and trashed her reputation. But she was signing a modeling contract almost the next day, from the sound of it. She basically cut off a lot of friends and professional acquaintances and vanished."

The pieces were slowly coming together. Abby recalled what Gabrielle had told her, and the sheer desperation on her face when she talked about what she'd been forced to give up.

"Look, this stays between us, right?" she said.

Nathan said, "Of course," and Jason nodded solemnly.

Abby outlined what she knew about Gabrielle's relationship with her manager, the way he'd manipulated her and forced her into contracts she hadn't wanted, had burned bridges behind her and effectively trapped her in a career she wasn't thrilled with, tying her to him.

When she finished, Nathan looked grim. "You think that's why she got the reputation of the Ice Queen?"

"I think that's a defense mechanism," Abby said. "Darren is using her for his own gain, and sabotages any attempts she makes to make connections or have a personal life. He wants her powerless, and unable to escape the web he's woven for her. So if she's cold to everyone around her, she doesn't form attachments, and no one else can get close enough to hurt her or be hurt."

"How financially stable is she, if she cuts all ties?" Jason asked.

Nathan had mentioned that he was an investment broker, so it made sense that he'd latch on to the financial aspect. "I'm not sure." Gabrielle had paid for her father's bills. She'd also mentioned that the cancer was back; was she sending him money again, or would he expect her to continue doing so? Or had Darren once again interfered and offered on her behalf? *There are too many unknowns.* "I get the impression that she's doing really well modeling. But she also has some expenses that she may need to cover... I'm not entirely sure. And how much of that would she keep if she broke her contract with Darren?" She shrugged. "I know Gabrielle wants to keep working. She dreams of going back to theater, but the fear is that Darren has trashed her reputation too much and no one will touch her now."

Nathan tapped his lip while he thought. "I can talk to a few people. You remember Tony, right?" Abby nodded. It wasn't every day that she was asked out by a handsome man while being twirled around the dance floor. "He knows a lot of people in the theater world. If I ask, he might put a few feelers out, maybe start a few rumors to fight the ones already out there."

"That would be amazing. Thank you. I just want her free from Darren. You should have seen him the first time he came storming in while we were in the middle of a date. He was furious that she was taking time to herself, that she'd chosen to go on a date instead of a business meeting he'd arranged. He's vindictive, conniving, and manipulative." She sketched out the events from the photoshoot, and how Darren had approached her when she'd been alone to try and drive a wedge between her and Brie.

"Did he hurt you?" Nathan sat up straight. "Or Gabrielle?"

"No, I get the impression that he's less about fists and more about cutting words. He's a total Slytherin."

That got a brief laugh from both Nathan and Jason.

"I'll do what I can," Nathan promised. "If there's a way to help Gabrielle get away from him then we'll find it."

With one problem being looked into, Abby turned her attention to the second problem in her life. She interviewed with a library in Hoboken, although she desperately did not want to commute across to New Jersey every day. She emailed people at libraries in and around the city. She even spoke with a woman she'd met at a librarian conference once, who worked up in Yonkers. Nothing panned out.

As May turned into June, Abby's desperation started to grow.

"Two weeks to go," Brian said grimly on Wednesday morning.

Marcy knocked him on the back of the head as she passed. "None of that," she said. "Counting down the days is just going to make everyone more miserable."

"I thought you had a possible position in Queens?" Abby asked him once Marcy had vanished into her office.

Brian shrugged. "They aren't sure they're going to fill the position after all. How's your search going?"

"About as well as yours. Interviewed with a branch in Jersey, but we'll see what comes of that."

They fell into silence, working with stubborn determination to ignore the upsetting possibility of unemployment. Their smiles to patrons were a bit too bright, movements a tiny bit too forceful, but Abby realized as the afternoon wound down that there was also a strange sense of comradery; they were all in this together.

While she didn't have many friends, Abby had always relied on Brian, Marcy, and the library to be a steady constant in her life. Losing her job was going to be incredibly painful, but losing the people she worked with every day was going to make it even worse.

"Hey." She looked over at Brian, "We should keep in touch. When all of this is over."

Brian seemed surprised. "Really?"

"Yeah." Abby shrugged. "I know I keep to myself a lot. I don't socialize out of work really. But I've been realizing lately that I need more good people in my life. And I'm going to miss you and Marce and all of the regulars once they close the branch."

Brian reached over, squeezing her shoulder gently. "Sure," he said. "Let's plan to get drinks on the last day. I'll let Marcy know too, and the other ladies."

Her frustration and anger and hopelessness were still there, but Abby was able to smile, and the rest of the afternoon passed by in a relaxed silence.

Gabrielle called her that evening, effectively erasing the last dregs of the black mood she'd sunk into during the day.

"Brie."

"I miss you," Gabrielle said.

Abby smiled into the phone. "I miss you too," she said. "Today was a bad one, I wish I could have come home and curled up in your arms after."

"I can get in a cab right now, just give me the word."

It was already getting late, and as tempting as the offer was, Abby couldn't accept.

"What if we get dinner tomorrow night?" she asked instead.

Gabrielle made a low groan. "I can't tomorrow."

She didn't need to say anything else. Abby was beginning to know her well enough to understand what that voice meant.

"Friday then?"

Gabrielle was silent for a moment. "Yes. I can do Friday."

Abby hesitated. "Brie, are you sure?"

This time Gabrielle sounded confident when she responded. "Absolutely. Dinner. Perhaps somewhere more relaxed than Printemps?"

"Yes, please!" Abby laughed, her hesitation washing away. She was secretly relieved that Gabrielle had noticed how uncomfortable she'd been at the expensive restaurant, and comforted that she was making an effort to help Abby feel at ease.

"I'll text you tomorrow with a restaurant," Gabrielle said.

They talked for a bit longer, and then Abby reluctantly hung up the phone, wishing fiercely that it was already Friday. Gabrielle had become a shining beacon in her life, especially as the library—formerly a haven and spot of joy in her day—was becoming something that inspired dread and restless nights.

Nathan had told her to find a reason to keep going when things seemed bleak. Life seemed pretty damn bleak right then, and it looked like she was going to be out of her dream job in only two more weeks. But Gabrielle was definitely a reason to keep going.

"But I need to tell her the truth first," Abby said, as though speaking the words out loud would make them easier to swallow. "I'll tell her at dinner on Friday."

Abby checked the text on her phone, and compared it to the numbers on the building in front of her. They matched, but when Gabrielle had mentioned a more laid-back restaurant for dinner, Abby had not expected this.

There was a door with a small sign and an old-fashioned wrought iron lamp above it, tucked into a quiet side-street in midtown. It was a literal hole-in-the-wall, and only the obvious care taken with the building and door—no graffiti, everything looking clean and new—gave Abby the confidence to push the door open.

Inside was a totally different story. The lights were dim and the walls painted in muted colors, creating an intimate feeling throughout the restaurant. And it *was* a restaurant; she could smell something delicious coming from the back, and there were people tucked into private booths as a hostess led her through a winding series of hallways until she spotted Gabrielle.

It was the complete opposite of Printemps. Instead of the almost sterile environment of bright candlelight, expensive furnishings, and obvious wealth, this restaurant was inviting, but also private. The wealth was still there, in the expensive wood and soft fabric of the tablecloths, the clearly decadent meals she'd glimpsed on other people's tables as she'd been walking.

"Do you like it?" Gabrielle asked, rising to greet her with a kiss.

Abby returned the gesture, smiling as she looked around. "I do. How'd you find it?"

"It is a members-only club," Gabrielle said. "You must be invited the first time by another member, after which you may be extended the opportunity to apply for membership of your own." She took Abby's hand in her own, refusing to let go even as they sat across from each other, their entwined fingers resting on the table between them. "You seem tired."

"I've been struggling this week," Abby admitted. "The library will be closing in two weeks, and I haven't managed to find another position yet."

Gabrielle ran her thumb over the soft skin of Abby's inner wrist, the gesture soothing. "What do you plan to do then?"

Abby shrugged. "I think they'll give us some kind of package for letting us go," she said. "Maybe a month or two of wages, but it won't be enough to cover rent and cost of living for long. I can keep searching, or just start applying for some kind of administrative role."

Gabrielle made a thoughtful sound. "But they're definitely closing the library you work at?" she said.

"They're meeting to vote on June 15," Abby said. "But it's pretty much certain they'll vote yes. We'll be closing within a few days after that, I guess." She shook her head. "Let's talk about something more pleasant."

"Let me tell you my plan for after dinner then," Gabrielle said, eyes brightening.

"Does it involve chocolate?"

Gabrielle smiled. "It could," she said. "If it means getting to see that expression of pure satisfaction on your face again." She fiddled with her wine glass, smiling. "After, I would like to take you back to my home."

And have sex, Abby finished in her head.

But Gabrielle didn't continue the way Abby had expected. "I would like to put on a movie in the background that we have both seen a dozen times, and curl up with you on the couch, and hold you for a few hours." She paused, then grinned. "And possibly feed you chocolate while we lay on the couch together."

"You want to cuddle" Abby said.

"Yes."

Abby found herself smiling. "That sounds perfect."

Gabrielle hesitated, then added, "And I would like very much if you would stay the night," She seemed hesitant, and it took Abby by surprise. "I would like to wake up tomorrow with you in my arms. Make breakfast with you. Perhaps curl up and read the paper together, trading sections as we finish them."

Habit from previous boyfriends and girlfriends meant Abby was processing excuses before Gabrielle had finished speaking; she'd become adept at worming out of situations where she'd be expected to have sex. *I could tell her that I can't, because I didn't bring a change of clothes, or I have plans in the morning with friends.* But she shoved aside the automatic reaction and let the fantasy sweep through her, grinning by the end of it. "Yes. I would love that too."

Warmth ignited in Abby's chest as she stared at Gabrielle. *Is this what love feels like?* Having someone to smile with, to laugh with, to want to spend all of her time with? She'd watched Gabrielle unfold like a flower blossom since they met, from the hard statue that had earned a nickname like The Ice Queen. Now Gabrielle was looking Abby with eyes that shined with happiness in the candlelight, her entire body relaxed. She'd opened up, and become someone that Abby wanted to spend every second of every day with.

Now was the time. Now, when they were planning their night together, and Gabrielle would continue to smile that beautiful smile and everything would be just as perfect as the evening laid out before them. "Brie," Abby began, "I want to tell—

But Gabrielle wasn't looking at her. In a split-second, her gaze had shifted to a point over Abby's shoulder, and the warmth had fled, her shoulders going up and her eyes turning hard, like chips of obsidian.

"Brie?"

"Excuse me for just one moment, Abigail," Gabrielle said. She was standing before Abby could respond, and her chin was up, shoulders back, like she was walking into war.

Abby spun in her seat, but there was no sign of whatever had triggered the sudden change in Gabrielle's demeanor. Just the restaurant, its labyrinth of corridors and tiny spots of light in the dimness.

Abby went to pick up her water glass, and realized her hands were shaking. She'd worked herself up to that moment, to telling Gabrielle the truth, and then Gabrielle had vanished before she could finish her sentence.

She carefully placed her napkin on the table, pushed her chair back, and stood on unsteady legs. A waiter appeared quickly, and Abby waved him off with a smile that probably looked more pained than genuine.

"We'll return in a moment," she said.

She had no idea where Gabrielle had vanished to, but she wandered through the restaurant until she was approaching the kitchens. Was there a bathroom down here that Gabrielle had ducked into?

Abby almost turned to head back to the table, but the murmur of muted voices permeated the silence. The restaurant was clearly designed to muffle any sounds, allowing for maximum privacy, but these were coming from just around the corner and it was obvious that the speakers were doing so in anger by the elevated tones she could just make out.

Abby stuck her head around the corner, and froze.

Gabrielle was leaning against the wall, arms crossed beneath her breasts, chin up, haughty and refusing to bow down. And in front of her was Darren, standing only inches from her, so close that they were surely sharing body heat.

"You shouldn't be here," Gabrielle was saying. Her voice was cold enough to sting, and if looks could kill then Darren would be six feet under right then.

"I'm the one who got you membership here, if you'll recall." Darren didn't appear angry. He sounded calm, like someone discussing the weather.

Gabrielle waved her hand dismissively, almost hitting Darren in the face. "You got me nothing," she said. "Everything I've accomplished, I did on my own."

"By sleeping with whoever you needed to?"

Gabrielle's chin jutted up. "If that's what it took."

Abby pressed her body into the wall, feeling small.

"What are you getting out of the mousy little bitch at the table then?" Darren's head was tilted to the side, and even though his voice was calm, his entire body was coiled like a snake about to strike. He was dangerous.

Gabrielle laughed, a hollow, humorless noise. "The best thing of all, of course."

"You're sleeping with her to get back at me." The words were low, hinting toward anger, and Abby had to struggle to hear him. "We both know it. This is your petty revenge scheme . . . and let me tell you, it's pathetic. When are you going to stop slumming it and grow up?" He took a half-step closer, so that they were chest to chest. Gabrielle was an inch taller than him, but she suddenly looked shorter as he seemed to loom over her.

"So what if I am?" Gabrielle asked. "There's nothing you can do about it. Everyone knows now. The reporters saw us at dinner, and the entire modeling community is abuzz after I brought her to the set. They know that I would rather 'slum it' with a nobody than sleep with you."

Abby's chest was tight, her lungs refusing to expand and contract.

She pushed off the wall before she could hear anything else, and blindly made her way back to the table. She found her purse, then turned before she could second-guess herself and hurried out of the restaurant. The alley was quiet, but the city was loud around her.

"I can't be here," she whispered, and fled.

chapter

Twenty-One

S he didn't have the money, now more than ever, but a cab seemed like the only option. Sitting on a train for half an hour, surrounded by crowds of people who were happy, enjoying their Friday night, was an impossible task. She waved down a taxi as soon as she got out to the street, sliding into the back and stuttering over her address.

Her phone vibrated in her bag. She didn't answer it.

Had she seen this coming? Abby remembered the first time they'd met, Gabrielle turning her around the dance floor. She'd talked then about getting back at him someday, and had smiled at Abby like she was the answer to all of her problems. And after Darren had ambushed Abby at the photoshoot, hadn't Gabrielle said that she was working on a way to get revenge on him for everything he'd done to her?

Abby had been blind. She'd let her feelings for Gabrielle consume her, and had forgotten that Gabrielle was the Ice Queen.

As they drove over the bridge into Brooklyn, she had a moment of panic.

"I changed my mind," she told the driver, and rattled out a different address.

By the time the cab pulled up to the front of her destination, she was shaking with the tears she refused to spill. She pushed open the door of the apartment building, stumbled upstairs, found the door purely by luck, and knocked.

Sara answered, frowning in confusion. Her face shifted to worry when she saw Abby standing there. "What's wrong?"

Abby stumbled in, and Sara caught her, closing the door and helping her to the couch. Safely ensconced in the cushions, and with Sara next to her as a comforting weight, she let the words and tears overflow, sobbing over the events of the night.

When the words dried up—though the tears did not—Sara was silent.

"I guess she earned the nickname," she said at last.

Abby nodded miserably.

"Oh, sweetie, I'm so sorry," Sara said, and pulled her into a hug, letting her cry onto her shoulder.

Abby's body gave out before the tears did, and she woke the next morning on Sara's couch with her eyes feeling like sandpaper and her entire body hurting. *I must have fallen asleep on Sara's shoulder.*

"Oh, you're awake." Nathan wandered into the room, apparently perfectly at home with a cup of coffee in hand.

"What are you doing here?" Abby asked.

He set the cup down and slid onto the couch, lifting her feet so he could sit and resettling them on his lap. "Got a call from Sara right after last night's performance ended, telling me she had a distraught woman on her couch. You were out for the count when I finally got here, so I crashed in my old room."

"Sorry to make you come all the way out here," she whispered.

"Hey." Nathan gripped her leg, forcing her attention to him. "Don't apologize for this. This is what friends are for, and I'd do it again in a heartbeat if you ever needed me."

Something shifted inside Abby. The tears were gone, and her body felt wrung out, but she located the sensation and realized it was warmth and comfort, the result of having people she could trust and count on. "I trusted her," she said. "I was about to tell her about being asexual, about how much I loved being around her, and then she . . ." Maybe the tears weren't entirely gone after all.

Nathan nodded. "You fell hard, and you fell fast. Trust me, I know how that feels. And I know that the heartbreak of losing that person is like your soul being torn in half."

Sara came out with her own cup of coffee, and perched on the end of the coffee table. "Your phone kept buzzing," she told Abby, handing her a cup of coffee. "I ended up turning it off."

She didn't need to say who had called. Abby could figure that out by the tightness of Sara's eyes, and the pressed line of her lips.

"Thank you." Abby sat up to take a sip. "Oh, this is the good stuff," she said, the flavor hitting her tongue.

Nathan smiled. "I ran out this morning and got a pound of the really good beans. It was either that or ice cream for breakfast." At Abby's raised eyebrow, he elaborated. "I stopped on my way over last night to pick up ice cream, because I've been assured," he nodded to Sara, "that ice cream is the most appropriate food for when a girl has a bad break-up. But you were already asleep, and ice cream didn't seem like an appropriate breakfast food.'"

"Pretty sure ice cream is an anytime emotional-crutch food," Abby said, and while she wasn't smiling yet, her body was starting to let go of the tension and the pain she'd held all night.

Sara jumped to her feet. "Ice cream for breakfast, then?"

"I can support that," Nathan agreed. He glanced at Abby

Abby nodded, and finally felt the edges of her mouth curl up slightly.

"Thank you," she said. "For being here."

Sara pressed a kiss on the top of her head, then vanished into the kitchen. "That's what friends are for," she called.

They spent the morning on Sara's couch, eating chocolate ice cream and sipping expensive coffee, watching animated movies with happy endings until Abby was no longer at risk of splintering apart.

By the time she got home that night, Jenna was waiting for her, sitting on the couch with the TV on low and muting it entirely as Abby walked in. "You weren't answering your phone."

Abby realized she hadn't ever turned it back on, but couldn't find it in her to feel guilty. She'd needed the solace, the little den of friendship and warmth that Nathan and Sara had created for her that day.

Jenna followed her as Abby kicked off her shoes and hung up her purse. "Everything alright?"

Abby nodded at Jenna. "Yeah," she said, "I think everything is going to be okay."

She could survive this.

Famous last words, Abby thought several days later.

She took another look around the breakroom and sighed. Marcy had started to dismantle all of the non-essential parts of the library in advance. Once the library was closed, a team of movers would come for the books and shelves, and they'd eventually be sold off or distributed to other branches. But the rest of the library was theirs to pack away or throw out.

Things had not gotten better. It had been a week since she'd left Gabrielle at the restaurant with Darren, and she'd finally settled on a single emotion that burned through her chest whenever she thought of the other woman: betrayal.

"It's ironic," she'd told Nathan, stretching her legs out on the table while watching the TV screen the weekend before. "Gabrielle always talked about how she was betrayed by Darren, how she'd loved him and he'd twisted that love into something he could use."

Nathan had frowned. "She did to you exactly what he did to her," he'd said, and had given her a sideways hug. "She was so caught up in trying to get her revenge on Darren, to get back at him, that she made herself just like him."

And that betrayal had kept Abby upright and moving for the last week. She'd gone to work, resolute in standing tall, in refusing to let Gabrielle's actions and words hurt. She'd gone home in the evenings and ignored her phone, which had eventually fallen silent at the end of the weekend, and had found strength in knowing she could be better, stronger, and not let the betrayal knock her down.

But deep down inside, she wanted Gabrielle to apologize. She watched romantic comedies on TV in the evening, where a guy would stand beneath a girl's window to shout his love. And she daydreamed about her favorite stories, longing for Gabrielle to appear and make things right again. Abby had checked out a few of her favorite romance novels from the library, and spent a few nights reading over the tales of heartbreak and misunderstandings, which always had Happily Ever Afters by the last page.

Gabrielle knew where she lived, and where she worked. The last time Abby had ignored her calls, Brie had shown up at her work and apologized in person. Yet now Gabrielle was absent. There had been no flowers, no surprise visits. Her now-silent phone had been a relief only until Abby had realized it was really the end of their relationship.

I guess she didn't care after all.

It was all the proof she needed. As much as it hurt to admit it to herself, Gabrielle had only been using her. Maybe there had been affection, but in the end Gabrielle had gotten what she wanted from the relationship, and now she was moving on.

I hope, at least, that she was able to defeat Darren. If Abby was going to be heartbroken and hurt, she couldn't help but want that pain to serve some other purpose. Maybe this had been the push Gabrielle needed, to get Darren to back down.

As the days passed, Abby had stopped checking her phone every few minutes. She'd stopped opening the door to the apartment in hope, waiting to find a long white box of flowers beneath her mailbox. She'd stopped glancing up when the door to the library opened, waiting to see glowing eyes and dark hair.

In a way, she realized, she'd followed Gabrielle's own example: she'd hardened her heart, found the chinks in her armor and fortified them, and made herself stronger, erecting a barrier to hide from the pain..

It didn't make things better, though. It just made them more bearable.

And now, standing in the library and knowing that the fate of their library was going to be signed away in only five days, a sliver of pain that managed to slip through her newly-formed walls.

Throughout the week people had come up to her and said they were writing their council members, protesting the closure. Abby had done all the right things; she'd smiled, nodded, encouraged them, commiserated. But she'd been numb beneath that outer layer.

It took her a moment to register that she wasn't alone in the room. Brian had walked in while she'd been thinking, and Abby turned toward him as he stopped at her side. "It hurts more, seeing it like this," Brian said. He gestured to the empty bulletin boards, the kitchenette area where they'd stashed coffee and tea. "I don't think it became real in my mind until I started seeing the blank spaces were the library used to exist."

They had a story time happening in half an hour, but Abby wasn't sure she could swallow around the lump in her throat to read to the children. "Can you take the story time today?"

He nodded, eyes understanding. "It's gonna get better."

"Yeah, when?"

Brian shrugged. "I don't know, but it always does."

She'd been a librarian for years, had wanted to be a librarian since she was old enough to understand what libraries were.

"Hey." Brian sounded cheerful. "Congrats to your lady."

Abby glanced toward him, frowning. "What do you mean?"

"I saw in the Arts section today. She's joined the ensemble for Hamilton. That's pretty huge, right?"

Abby felt the chinks in her armor grow wide, and quickly shoved everything she could into plugging them up. "We're not together anymore." She was proud that she'd succeeded in keeping her voice level.

"Oh." Brian blinked, opening his mouth and closing it again. "Sorry."

"It happens," Abby said, shrugging. *Calm calm calm,* she whispered in her head. "But that's good to hear. I knew she'd wanted to get back on stage."

Brian clearly wasn't sure what to say, and he exhaled, then turned to leave Abby alone. He paused though, then leaned over and gave her a hug. "I'm sorry."

Abby stood straight until he was gone, then let her shoulders hunch in.

So Gabrielle had accomplished it: she'd gotten back to the stage. Was this part of her plan to get back at Darren? Had she managed to create enough distance between them that she could break free? And had Nathan's friend Tony come through and helped her out?

"It's over," she said. "Gabrielle can go on with her life. I'll go on with mine."

It was okay, she reasoned. Gabrielle was destined for the stage, and Abby was just a bookworm. A soon-to-be-unemployed bookworm. In spite of the things they'd had in common, their shared interests, they were two very different people. Abby had risked her heart for Gabrielle, and in the end Gabrielle had been exactly as advertised.

They probably wouldn't have worked out anyways.

She took two deep breaths, then squared her shoulders and went back to boxing up the signs, posters, and little touches that had made the library her home for the last few years.

chapter

Twenty-Two

The morning of the fifteenth started with a heat-wave that made everything feel like it was moving in slow motion. Summer had been slow to settle in, but Abby woke up sticky from the humidity and knew it was going to be a hot one that day.

She helped Jenna wrestle the air conditioner unit into the window before getting dressed and heading to work.

The library was thankfully nice and cool, but the look on Marcy and Brian's faces when they all sat down for their morning meeting was enough to chill Abby right to the bone.

"The city council are voting today," Marcy said.

Abby nodded. She hadn't forgotten, but had tried to push the thought aside. The last few days had been a frantic push to find a new position, but there was nothing. The other branches that were closing, combined with a city-wide cut of labor and hours, meant Abby was in trouble.

Her mother was trying to get her to move back out to Long Island when her lease with Jenna ended in September. Abby had gone out to brunch with her parents the previous weekend, and had managed to avoid talking about Gabrielle and their now non-existent relationship by using the library as a conversation point instead. Her mother had said she could find office work and live rent free there.

The thought was less than appealing.

"When's the vote?" Brian asked.

"Ten o'clock," Marcy said. "We should have information by the end of the day about the closing timeline, but I'm guessing we'll have until next week."

Abby sat in silence, letting Marcy and Brian talk about how the closures would probably play out.

Then they had to go to work, opening the library like normal, smiling like normal, checking books out and helping with recommendations like normal. *Is this how Nathan feels when he's on stage, pretending to be someone else and putting on a face that didn't match what you're feeling inside?*

Mostly, Abby felt empty.

Ten o'clock came and went. Abby could see the stress lines forming on Marcy's face as they didn't get any news by eleven, then noon. Just before lunch, Marcy made a phone call, then came back out. "They're still in council session."

"What's taking so long?" Abby asked.

Marcy shrugged. "I don't know. I wish they'd just get it over with though."

Abby ate her sandwich for lunch, read part of a new book, and forced herself not to think about the council vote.

When she stood to go back to work an hour later, Marcy was leaning against the breakroom door with a strange look on her face.

"Got the call," she said.

Abby nodded, her food sitting like a rock in her stomach.

Marcy was studying her. "Who do you know? Did you plan this?"

"What?" Abby blinked, but Marcy's face didn't offer up any explanation. "Plan what?"

"The council voted," Marcy said. "They're not closing us down."

It took a minute for Abby to process those words.

"What?" she repeated.

Marcy shook her head slowly. It was clear she was still trying to absorb the news as well. "Some wealthy donor got up at the council meeting and pled for the library to stay open. Got a bunch of other people there too, and they offered donations and convinced the council that we were essential."

"That's . . . that's amazing," Abby breathed.

"And they kept bringing up your name."

The words were dropped into the silence, and Abby took a step back. "My name?"

"Yeah, that's the strangest part. Somehow a bunch of rich old folks in Manhattan are suddenly concerned about a small library branch in

Brooklyn, and they're citing your name to the council? You must have friends in high places." Marcy was still watching her, like she'd never seen Abby before.

Abby shook her head. "I don't know anyone like that."

But that wasn't true, and her expression must have shifted, because Marcy nodded.

"Whoever it was, you thank them for me. I've gotta go tell Brian and the rest of the staff. We're not out of the woods yet; they're still gonna shift our budget around, but we're staying open."

Abby waited until Marcy had left, and then sunk back into her seat.

Gabrielle had done this. It was the only answer possible. Nathan knew people, but not anyone who could have this kind of pull, and Jason's circle of wealth was totally different. It had to be Gabrielle.

But why had she done this? After betraying Abby and leaving her heartbroken and used, what had prompted her to gather people she knew and convince them to save the library? Was this a 'thank you' for unintentionally helping her to get back at Darren? Or something else entirely?

Abby needed answers.

She knocked on Gabrielle's apartment door that evening, a quick rap before she could chicken out and flee the building.

There was no answer.

She didn't know when Gabrielle might be home. Maybe she was working, or out with other people. Maybe she was at the theater she was going to be performing at? Abby backtracked to the front of the building, and found a bench by the nearest bus stop. It was still fairly warm, but the sun was starting to vanish behind the buildings and it was comfortable to sit there. She pulled a book out of her bag and settled in to wait until Gabrielle came home.

She must have been sitting there for a couple of hours, because the sun was low on the horizon and the entire city was orange and pink.

"I've read that one," a voice said.

Abby looked up to see Gabrielle standing in front of her.

"Any good?"

Gabrielle nodded. "Yes, but the sequel is even better."

"We only have the first one at our library," Abby said.

"I can lend it to you." Gabrielle paused, uncharacteristically hesitant. "If you would like, that is."

Abby used her finger as a bookmark and studied Gabrielle, backlit by the stunning orange sunset. She seemed tired, but still as beautiful as the first time Abby had seen her. "I wanted to say thank you in person," Abby said. "For what you did to save the library."

Gabrielle nodded. "I would have done anything I could to see that darkness and weight lifted from your shoulders." She shifted, and Abby realized suddenly that she was nervous. "Would you like to come up?"

"Are you actually going to answer my questions, instead of avoiding them like you've done before?"

Gabrielle didn't answer, but her shoulders went tense in a way that Abby had grown to recognize.

"I overheard you and Darren at the restaurant that night," she said.

Gabrielle jerked. "Abigail."

But Abby wasn't done. She crossed her ankles, leaning back against the bench to better watch Gabrielle. "I'm not going to lie and say that it doesn't hurt, knowing you were using me to get back at your manager. The days after I heard you two talking were probably some of the roughest I've ever faced. But I've accepted it and moved on. You've taught me a lot about putting a wall between yourself and the world."

Gabrielle's body tensed more and more with every sentence, her eyes filling until tears spilled over. It wasn't something Abby had ever seen on her; she'd seen Gabrielle angry, happy, cold, and seductive, but she'd never seen her cry.

"I think we need to have that talk," Gabrielle said in a small voice. "I would like to tell you something. Even if it does nothing to change your mind, I would ask for a few minutes of your time in the hopes that I can make this right."

Abby rubbed her finger over the pages of her books, letting the feel of the paper soothe her. "I'll listen, but . . . I also need answers," she said. "You saved my job, and I'm grateful. But I can't . . . I need to know why." She tucked the paperback into her bag and stood, aware of how close it suddenly brought her to Gabrielle.

Gabrielle's shoulders slumped with relief. "I will tell you everything you want to know. Please, come up."

The inside of the apartment was not how Abby expected. She'd been there twice now, but gone were the clean lines and the shining chrome surfaces. Now it was filled with boxes and packing materials, furniture wrapped up and set against the wall.

"You're moving," she said.

Gabrielle nodded. "I have some money saved from modeling, but not much. The lawsuit with Darren will likely exhaust my savings, so it is time for me to find somewhere else to live."

Abby paused by a pile of boxes marked BOOKS. "So you're firing him."

"I already have." Gabrielle's smile was triumphant. "The night you witnessed us in the restaurant in fact. You made me realize that I didn't need to suffer any longer, that I could take action. I could either live my life in fear, and let Darren continue to rule over my every movement, or I could break free and find my own path."

"What about your father?"

Gabrielle's shoulders slumped. She didn't look sad, however, merely resigned. "He will likely pass away very soon. The cancer, it is resisting all treatment. The doctor says he has only weeks."

Abby opened her mouth to say *Sorry*, but something about Gabrielle's posture said empty sympathies wouldn't be welcome. "Are you going to be okay?" she asked instead.

"Yes. I am upset, of course. He is my father, even if we don't get along. He married my mother because she was beautiful, but he never loved her, or me. And I'm not sure that what I feel for him is love. Gratitude, for raising me, and because of that I have made sure to set aside money to cover any extra costs to make his last few weeks comfortable. I will be sad when he passes, but I think . . ." Her voice dropped. "I think also relieved."

There was silence between them.

"So you're free then. From Darren, from his webs. You have a job in theater."

Gabrielle's smile was barely-there, but genuine. "Yes."

"I'm glad," Abby said.

The silence this time was awkward. Abby was tempted to start asking her questions, could feel them all bubbling up in her chest, eager to escape. But there was one she needed an answer to more than the others. "Was anything between us real? Or was it all to get back at Darren?"

Gabrielle's eyes closed. "The answer to that question is more complicated than a *yes* or a *no*." She motioned to the couch, one of the few items that had not been wrapped up or boxed yet. "Please, let me explain."

Abby settled on the edge of the cushion, putting as much room between them as she could. She folded her hands in her lap so she wouldn't fidget with them, and waited.

"My entire adult life, people have wanted something from me," Gabrielle began. "Sometimes they wanted to use me, or control me—beauty is a commodity to many people. Mostly, though, they wanted sex."

There was that word, the entire reason Abby had been hesitant to push her relationship with Gabrielle forward. She swallowed and bit her lip. Gabrielle was giving her answers at last, and she wasn't going to interrupt now and risk missing out on the story she so desperately wanted to hear.

"I met Darren, and he was the first person who wanted me for *me*, not for my looks or my body. At least, that's what I thought. At first everything was perfect. I loved him."

"But he betrayed you." Abby interrupted, then immediately regretted it.

Gabrielle nodded. "He was not always cruel, but the promise of money can make a man like Darren was change. Eventually he found it to be a better alternative to love. I was offered a modeling contract by a small but well-known fashion house. I turned down the offer, but Darren saw the contract—he saw the amount being offered, I should say—and begged me to reconsider. He was very persuasive, but I wasn't ready to give up on my passion for acting, and he quickly realized that it was a dead-end."

Abby glanced over to the kitchen. She hadn't checked the fridge when she walked in, but she guessed the picture of Gabrielle, her father and Darren still hung there.

"But instead of letting it go, he began to work behind the scenes, and soon negotiated an even bigger, more lucrative contract with a more reputable designer. I suspect that at first he convinced himself that he was doing what was best for both of us. But he knew I wouldn't agree. So when I told him about my father's cancer, I think he saw his chance. He didn't have access to my accounts, but he didn't need them; all he needed to do was invite my father to visit."

Gabrielle paused.

"He made you give money to your father." Abby had heard that part of the story, but now the details were coming to light.

"Yes." Gabrielle laughed, a low, tired sound. "I arrived at the restaurant thinking it was a date, that Darren was going to congratulate me on being offered the lead in *Chicago*. Instead, my father was at the table. And Darren took my hand, smiled at my father like they were old friends, and offered him a sum of money that I could not afford. He backed me into a corner until I found myself with no choice but to accept the modelling contract and turn down a role on Broadway that I'd long dreamed of."

Abby watched as Gabrielle stared at her hands, eyes wet with the memory and the loss.

"At first I thought, *Okay. It is a one-time thing*. I reasoned that maybe Darren was trying to help, that he genuinely cared." She shook her head. "I was naïve. He trashed my name in the theater industry, while simultaneously handing me contracts for modeling partners. He took a percentage of what I made, and so he began to make more as I did."

This was the most Abby had ever heard Gabrielle say. She pressed her lips together, worried that to interrupt again would be to stop the story. But she reached out her hand, offering it to Gabrielle, and smiled encouragingly when Gabrielle took it with a grateful nod before glancing away again.

"I vowed, as time went on, that someday I would get back at Darren and find a way to get rid of him." Abby looked up sharply, but Gabrielle didn't seem to notice, too lost in her own thoughts. "Over the years, though, it became more and more difficult. And then I met you." She turned back to Abby now.

"What you said to Darren . . .."

"Was only aimed to hurt him," Gabrielle quickly said. "I never meant for you to hear that. I never would say anything to hurt you."

"You used me."

"No." Gabrielle squeezed her hand. "I fell in love with you."

Abby opened her mouth. Closed it. Felt goosebumps break out on her arms. "You what?" she breathed.

Gabrielle spoke the words slowly. "I fell in love with you," she repeated. "And when Darren brought you up, I knew I had to protect you from him. Telling him that you were only a pawn in my game against him was the best way to do that. He would have gone for my weakness, and I couldn't let him know that . . ." she paused.

"That what?" Abby asked.

"That you're my weakness. The only person who managed to break through the walls I'd put up." She took a deep breath, and let it out. Her dark eyes caught Abby's and held them. "I spent so long trying to get back at Darren. Coming up with plans, fighting each battle one day at a time and planning to win what I believed was a war. At the gala that first night, you were a small triumph. And oh," she smiled, "Darren was furious afterward. That I got to dance briefly with a beautiful woman was a bonus. I believed I could use you, could manage another victory against him if I asked you on a date to thank you, and knew that there would be people in Printemps who would spread the word of our dinner together."

Abby swallowed. "Oh." She realized she was gripping Gabrielle's hand so hard her fingers had turned white at her knuckles, and forced herself to relax. Gabrielle didn't seem to notice, or at least didn't appear to mind.

"But somewhere between our discussion about books, and your disregard for the glamor and the expensive food, it struck me that you were unique. Someone special. It was only after the photoshoot that I understood that my desire for vengeance was going to ruin the one thing that I wanted far more—you. I wanted to hurt Darren, but I did not want to do so at the cost of hurting you . . . though of course I already had. Because I had fallen in love with you."

Gabrielle waited, but Abby was still turning that revelation over in her head. But the longer Abby went without answering, the more disappointed she appeared.

"I understand if you do not—

"I need to tell you something." Abby took her hand back, and pushed her hands into her thighs, fingers balled into fists, and didn't look directly at Gabrielle.

Gabrielle sat back.

"I'm not sure we can be together. I was worried about it before I overheard your argument with Darren. I'd planned to tell you that night, actually, but, well . . ." she shrugged.

Gabrielle rocked back, eyes wide and face pale. Abby watched her out of the corner of her eye, afraid that if she looked over she'd lose her strength to keep speaking.

"I want to be your girlfriend," Abby said, "but I don't want to have sex with you."

The words hung between them in the empty apartment, and Abby's stomach knotted like it was going to rebel, nausea rising in the back of her throat.

Gabrielle's words were barely a whisper. "I don't understand.".

Abby found a patch of dirt on the carpet, likely from one of the movers who was working in the apartment, and focused on it.

"I'm asexual."

"I don't know what this means," Gabrielle said.

"It means I don't do sex." Abby paused, then shook her head. "No, that's wrong. That's what most people think, but it's not accurate. It means I don't feel sexual attraction to anyone. Including you."

Gabrielle shifted, and Abby risked a glance to see what she was doing. Her brow was furrowed, eyes narrowed in thought. "But we had sex," she said. "And we've spent time together, kissing, holding each other."

Abby nodded. "I like being close to you," she said. "I like holding you and being held, and I love when you kiss me until we're both out of breath. But I don't have want to have sex."

This time Gabrielle was silent for so long that Abby did have to look up.

"So it was a lie then," Gabrielle finally said.

"What was?"

Gabrielle seemed upset. "The night we spent in my bed. The way you brought me pleasure, like you cared about me. But you did not want to be doing that, and so it was a lie, what was between us."

Abby shook her head. "None of it was a lie," she said adamantly. "I don't enjoy sex, but I didn't mind doing that for you. It was ∴ . . a compromise. An act that you were craving, that I could give you, but I didn't need anything in exchange for it."

"But that's what sex is!" Gabrielle said, straightening. "People do not want sex without getting something in return. They want a favor, a signature on a contract, an orgasm."

Abby's voice was barely audible. "Oh Gabrielle," she said. "What did they do to you?"

Gabrielle's head turned sharply, and Abby could see tears in her eyes.

Abby remembered the rumors, the conversations she'd been witness to, people who used Gabrielle or who she used in return. "You did what you needed, to survive what Darren had pushed you into," she said finally. "But that's not what sex is. For most people, I think it's another level of intimacy, of trust. It's a way to show love. For me, it's a way that I can help you relax, and show you that I'm willing to meet you halfway in a relationship. Nothing more."

Gabrielle pushed herself up off the couch and stood, staring at the blank walls and clenching her fists at her side. "I need a moment," she said, and vanished from the room.

Abby sat back, stunned. "That was *not* the way I expected that to go," she said out loud.

c h a p t e r

Twenty-Three

For the second time, Abby found herself searching for Gabrielle. She wasn't in the bedroom, which was the first place Abby looked. Eventually she found her out on the balcony, elbows hooked on the railing and shoulders curved as she gazed out at the buildings.

"I don't particularly enjoy sex," Gabrielle said when Abby opened the sliding door. She didn't glance over, and Abby closed the door behind her and leaned against the glass.

"You enjoyed it with me, I thought." Had Abby misread Gabrielle's reactions that night? She only understood the appeal of sex on a physical level, and theoretically on an emotional one, but she'd definitely believed it was what Gabrielle had wanted.

Gabrielle shrugged one elegant shoulder. "I enjoyed it because I enjoyed being with you, and because I thought it was something *you* wanted. But now I find that I forced you into having sex that you didn't want, and I'm not sure how to react to that. It makes me no better than Darren, to have manipulated you like this."

"No!" Abby shouted the word, and Gabrielle's head whipped around to look at her. "You're not like Darren. Not in this. You didn't trick me into having sex with you." Her voice dropped, low and insistent. "I did want it. I mean, I wanted to help you out. To show you that I could give you what you wanted in a relationship."

"And what do *you* want?" The words were almost harsh, desperation tinging them.

Abby thought about the answer before speaking. "I want someone to hold, to trust. Someone who will hold my hand in public and spend time with me, who will talk about books over coffee and wrap their arms around me while we watch a movie. I want someone to kiss and to send flowers to and to come home after work to." She took a deep breath. "I want you to be that someone."

Gabrielle exhaled. "The first night we danced, I thought I would repay you with sex, because this is the easiest currency I understand. But we went out to dinner, and after you rebuffed my attempts to repay you. I was intrigued, I'll admit. That's why I asked for a second date; no one had ever turned me down before."

Abby finally pushed herself off the glass and stepped forward to wrap her arms around Gabrielle's waist, pressing against Gabrielle until they were back to chest and she could inhale Gabrielle's perfume, familiar in its spiciness.

"It was a relief," Gabrielle said.

"Because you don't like using sex as a currency?"

"Because sex is only currency to me. The act itself is pleasurable, yes. I still crave release, still feel the attraction. But the act itself only ever meant that someone wanted something from me, and so the thought of having sex with another person is almost intolerable. But you didn't want anything from me." Gabrielle relaxed back into Abby's arms, shifting until she could look over her shoulder and press a kiss to Abby's forehead.

Abby tilted her head up to return the kiss, ignoring the awkward angle. "Then tell me what you need from me. I've told you what I want, so now it's your turn."

Gabrielle closed her eyes and tilted her head back. "I want someone who doesn't see my job, but only me. Someone who will help me break free from the shell I've hidden under for so long. Someone who will wander bookshops and food festivals with me, and who will explore the world with me." She turned in Abby's arms. "I think that someone might be you."

Abby met her halfway in the kiss, soft and passionate and tinged with relief.

"Abigail," Gabrielle said, pulling back. "What you did for me that night? Would you do it again?"

"Yes, Brie," Abby said in a heartbeat. "If you needed it, I could do that for you."

"But you wouldn't enjoy it," Gabrielle clarified.

Abby shook her head. "I would enjoy the look on your face,

and the way you melted afterwards, and the knowledge that you got pleasure from it," she said. "And if you were to hold me after and curl around me while we slept? I would enjoy *that*."

"Yes," Gabrielle said, and kissed her again. "I can do that."

The last trace of Abby's fear and sadness faded away, , standing there in Gabrielle's arms. "Brie," she said, "I think I'd really like to finish our date now."

Gabrielle gave her a smile that could melt the polar ice caps and nodded. "Yes, I would enjoy that very much."

They put on a sci-fi movie that they'd both seen a dozen times before, laughing as they took turns quoting lines and talking about their favorite scenes. Abby laid length-wise on the couch with Gabrielle in front of her, her arm wrapped beneath Gabrielle's breasts and Gabrielle's fingers wrapped around her own.

"Where do we go from here?" Abby whispered.

Gabrielle shrugged in her arms. "We go wherever we want," she said. "Greece or Peru or Thailand. We explore the world together."

"Yes, yes, and yes." Abby huffed out a laugh. "I would go anywhere with you, Brie. To Antarctica or Timbuktu or the Moon. But I meant between us. Where does this relationship go?"

Gabrielle curled back into Abby, and Abby wrapped her arms more securely around Gabrielle. "I think we go forward one day at a time. This won't be easy. You've said before, I am no good at communicating. I need a push, and I need you to stay with me when I falter. I'll frustrate you, upset you, say things that might hurt you, though I will never do so intentionally."

"And you're okay with me?" Abby asked.

"I am more than okay with everything about you," Gabrielle confirmed.

"I meant with me being ace."

Gabrielle wriggled around until she was lying on her back, her head pillowed on Abby's arm, so Abby could gaze down at her. "My response doesn't change," she said. "I only want what makes you happy, what brings you satisfaction. And I've learned in my life that sex . . .

doesn't always do that." She looked Abby in the eye. "I will meet you halfway."

Abby kissed her, and the movie was forgotten about.

They spent the night lying in Gabrielle's bed, Gabrielle's leg thrown over Abby's thigh and Abby's hand wrapped around Brie's back, sliding up to find the smooth skin there. They traded kisses until they had to separate to breathe, and then talked until they fell into more kisses.

"I have to know," Abby said as midnight came and went. They were whispering, the covers pulled over their heads, creating an intimate private world with just the two of them. "How did you save the library?"

"Your friend Tony approached me. He said you had asked for a favor."

"To get you back into theater," Abby said.

"Yes." Gabrielle shared their conversation, explained how Tony had pulled strings and called in favors to get her an audition for an ensemble role, and how she'd turned to Tony and his theater connections in return when she was seeking help to save the library.

"He is very fond of you," Gabrielle said.

"He asked me out," Abby said. Gabrielle's eyebrows went up in surprise. "The night of the gala. It was the first night we'd met, and he danced with me before you did, then asked me out."

Gabrielle kissed her forehead. "I must be selfish and admit to being thankful you said no," she said. "But when I mentioned that I needed his help to save your job, he didn't hesitate to ask what he could do to help."

"I never expected the library to stay open," Abby admitted. "I thought for sure that it was a done deal. It never even occurred to me that it could be saved."

Gabrielle kissed her again. "If there is one thing that I learned from the last few years," she said, "it's that people with a lot of money love to throw it around. I had Tony speak with some of the people he met at the charity gala, and I approached several of the designers and artists I've worked with in the past."

"What did you tell them?" Abby couldn't imagine a way to convince a group of wealthy patrons to support a library in the middle of Brooklyn.

"That there was a woman I was falling in love with," Gabrielle said. When Abby's eyes went wide, she smiled. "Many of these people have known me for years as the Ice Queen. And it's true; I became cold and emotionless to maintain some semblance of control over my own life. But I realized that I didn't need to pretend anymore. The rumors were already flying that I had fired Darren, and I think the knowledge that there was someone out there who could get me to *feel* again was enough to make many of the people I met with support me."

"Are you seriously telling me that the power of love saved my library?"

Gabrielle laughed. *I could live a hundred years more and never get tired of that sound.* "Yes, just like something out of a novel."

"And a bunch of people agreed to give their time and money because of that?" Abby asked, disbelief in her voice.

Gabrielle kissed her again, and then again. "Abigail," she said between kisses. "You of all people should know how important stories are. The story of finding love and saving a library against overwhelming odds is the best kind of story."

"And does this story have a happily ever after?"

"Yes," Gabrielle said, and pulled Abby closer until there was no room left between them. "I think it does."

Explore more of the *Seasons of Love* series:
riptidepublishing.com/titles/universe/seasons-love

Dear Reader,

Thank you for reading Elyse Springer's *Thaw*!

We know your time is precious and you have many, many entertainment options, so it means a lot that you've chosen to spend your time reading. We really hope you enjoyed it.

We'd be honored if you'd consider posting a review—good or bad—on sites like **Amazon, Barnes & Noble, Kobo, Goodreads, Twitter, Facebook, Tumblr,** and your blog or website. We'd also be honored if you told your friends and family about this book. Word of mouth is a book's lifeblood!

For more information on upcoming releases, author interviews, blog tours, contests, giveaways, and more, please sign up for our weekly, spam-free newsletter and visit us around the web:

Newsletter: tinyurl.com/RiptideSignup
Twitter: twitter.com/RiptideBooks
Facebook: facebook.com/RiptidePublishing
Goodreads: tinyurl.com/RiptideOnGoodreads
Tumblr: riptidepublishing.tumblr.com

Thank you so much for Reading the Rainbow!

RiptidePublishing.com

Acknowledgments

There is no definitive 'asexual experience', and Abby's story is only meant to be one point on the asexuality spectrum.

I've made friends with some incredible people in the ace community over the last few years, who have helped me better understand asexuality as it applies to myself and to others. So thank you to Daniela, Michele, Erica, Danielle, and so many more for always being there to talk about asexuality. And to authors like Cass Lennox, TJ Klune, and others, who write gorgeous romances with ace characters, which allow me to see myself represented on the page.

A huge thank you to the incredible staff at Riptide for being so supportive of this book, and for giving Abby a home. And of course, thank you to Caz Galloway for being such a fantastic editor, and for understanding my obsession with *Harry Potter*.

You can learn more about asexuality at www.asexuality.org.

also by

Elyse Springer

Seasons of Love
Whiteout
Heat Wave (July 2017)
Changing Colors (October 2017)

Heels Over Head (May 2017)

about the *Author*

Elyse is an author and world-traveler, whose unique life experiences have helped to shape the stories that she wants to tell. She writes romances with LGBTQIA+ characters and relationships, and believes that every person deserves a Happily Ever After. When she's not staring futilely at her computer screen, Elyse spends her time adding stamps to her passport, catching up on her terrifying TBR list, and learning to be a better adult.

You can find her online at:
Website: elspringer.com
Twitter: @ElyseSpringer
Facebook: facebook.com/ElyseSpringerWrites

Enjoy more stories like
Thaw
at RiptidePublishing.com!

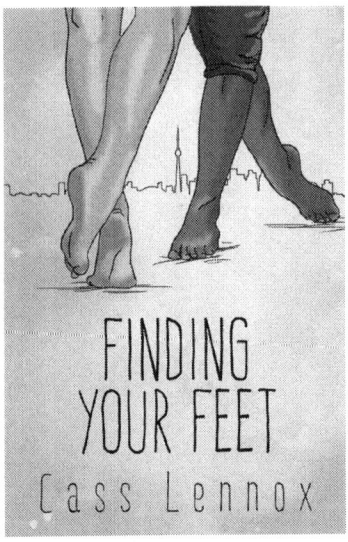

Finding Your Feet
ISBN: 978-1-62649-488-6

Far From Home
ISBN: 978-1-62649-452-7

Earn Bonus Bucks!

Earn 1 Bonus Buck for each dollar you spend. Find out how at
RiptidePublishing.com/news/bonus-bucks.

Win Free Ebooks for a Year!

Pre-order coming soon titles directly through our site and you'll
receive one entry into a drawing for a chance to win free books for
a year! Get the details at RiptidePublishing.com/contests.

65121383R00123

Made in the USA
Charleston, SC
15 December 2016